Lithium

Malén Denis

Lithium

translated by Laura Hatry
and John Wronoski

A NEW DIRECTIONS PAPERBOOK ORIGINAL

Originally published in Spain as *Litio* by Caballo de Troya / Penguin Random House. Published by arrangement with MB Agencia Literaria S. L.

Manufactured in the United States of America
First published as a New Directions Paperbook 1654 in 2026

Library of Congress Cataloging-in-Publication Data
Names: Denis, Malén, 1989– author | Hatry, Laura translator | Wronoski, John translator
Title: Lithium / Malén Denis ;
translated by Laura Hatry and John Wronoski.
Other titles: Litio. English
Description: New York : New Directions Publishing, 2026. | " A New Directions paperbook."
Identifiers: LCCN 2025053023 | ISBN 9780811239059 paperback | ISBN 9780811240314 ebook
Subjects: LCGFT: Fiction | Novels
Classification: LCC PQ7798.414.E65 L5813 2026
LC record available at https://lccn.loc.gov/2025053023

10 9 8 7 6 5 4 3 2 1

New Directions Books are published for James Laughlin
by New Directions Publishing Corporation
80 Eighth Avenue, New York 10011

Lithium (Greek: λιθίον, "little stone") is a silvery white alkali metal that is soft, ductile, and very light. It does not occur in a free state in nature, but only in compounds. It is used primarily in the production of heat-conducting alloys and electric batteries, and its salts have long been employed in the treatment of bipolar disorder.

Its density is half that of water, making it the lightest of the solid elements and metals. In its pure form, it oxidizes rapidly in air or water. When placed in proximity to flame it turns crimson, but in a more violent combustion reaction it flares a brilliant white.

WIKIPEDIA

Lithium

Below Zero

You were breathing fire when I met you, I should have sensed the danger: a pale, shirtless sixteen-year-old in the middle of a frozen field inhaling slugs of kerosene and spewing jets of flame out into the night. A layer of frost had dusted the grayish sedge, a faint thread of amber fluid writhed down the crease between your pecs. As you moved, light played over your body as if you'd just stepped out of a Vermeer. You seemed at home in the night and the outdoors, something of the woodsman about you, a sense of solving things by force, with the blow of an axe.

That winter they tried to convince me that cold is just a state of mind. It's a sensation, and sensations are psychological, some little Einstein who'd never heard of hypothermia blurted out at me. I didn't want to have to argue with a guy, besides, I would have given anything to stop shivering, so, sitting on a tree stump, huddled in my blue coat, I telepathically willed my body to conjure up some heat. You loved that coat, you said it was the exact color. The exact color of what, I never learned.

When I saw you walking in my direction I figured there must be someone standing right behind me. Are you drunk? you asked as your specter took on solid form. You wiped off your chest with a hand towel embroidered with an apple and something written in cursive. With one deft motion you pulled on a thick woolen sweater; it must have been itchy against your bare skin but you showed no sign of discomfort. You squinched your eyebrows, casting your face in shadow:

Don't do that anymore, you're not like those other girls, it doesn't suit you. I looked at you the way Sailor Moon looks at Tuxedo Mask, like a cute kitten from the Internet, a look with which you were already well acquainted.

I was captivated by your confidence in who you were. I was lucky if I could occasionally grasp a fleeting sense of myself from the contours of clothing against my flesh, but you were already wholly yourself, clearly cut out from your surroundings by a die you'd long since cast aside. You seemed to know a lot about everything. And what an honor to be different from "those other girls," though who they were I had no idea. And to be chosen to receive your words of advice, the joy that snapped through my body was an electric whip.

Touch

The sense of touch, how it works, has always intrigued me. You once told me that I couldn't tell how soft I was because the palms of my hands are so rough. Do you feel that? you said. First you made me touch your hand for comparison, waxy, like soap, and cool, like a fish. Yours are like paper, you decided. After that I had a hard time holding your hand.

The crux of the problem of touch arises when I'm trying to sense myself, to evaluate my own texture. Which part is doing the sensing then? How do I know what I really feel like? It's not a problem at every level, apart from my own body it's clear enough, and I can say unequivocally that this dress I'm wearing feels luscious, as soft and inviting as foam.

I try to recognize myself in the things I buy. Under the fitting room's mortuary glare I'm gray, shapeless, an orphaned World War II refugee. In moments like this the feeling that I have to fill up the time, the minutes, the hours, the time until whatever, descends upon me, and with it an urge to spend. And as always, trying not to be late, I end up being way too early. That's why I went into the shop in the first place, that and the air-conditioning.

Although there's something captivating in the image of me as a famished little orphan girl it's unlikely that I'll ever wear that light blue dress, the dress of a girl out browsing the meadows around your parents' house in search of greens for the evening meal. My mother used to say that we always look better in our own mirror, the one we've tamed, but the rest of them are wild, unpredictable—mirrors that recognize the beast in us.

The replica of *Guernica* in the lobby. I'm hoping that Delia will have the keys with her when she answers the door, though I already know that she won't and I'll have to go upstairs. In my mind I'm already there, I'm imagining the latest remodeling. They've knocked down a wall to enlarge the consulting room. Doubling the size, to be exact.

Reexamining the geometrical precision of the figures I always notice some new detail: a blade leaping maniacally from what seems to be the mouth of a furious horse. The same cold as always, the coolness of the marble, the catacomb of dark ceramic. The elevator, no one speaks. She immediately offers me a seat and brings a glass of water, remembering that my blood pressure tends to drop suddenly: It's important to stay hydrated in the summer.

I already have an inkling of how this will go. Your mother, like an actress entering her "living room scene," arms waving: Dear this, dear that, this situation, they didn't want to scare me, you asked for me but they think it's better if I don't go; Violeta has been "contained." A certain artificiality that I couldn't quite pin to anything specific, whether to the lexical choice of "contained" or to her movements, decisive but calculated, choreographed even, as if she knew just the right tincture of drama to inject. Violeta's with her parents, she won't be coming back, and the cats have had a litter.

I'm sitting on the edge of the armchair and fear that I'll leave a mark—I'm sweating and my bare legs are touching the leather, real leather. As you can imagine, she informs me, I can't bring the cats here; I'm never home and I can't force *her* (gesturing with her chin towards Delia), besides, I just got that new armchair. Her bracelets jingle as she adjusts a lock of hair that's fallen across the left side of her forehead: I have to get back to my patients, but you'll be able to manage, won't you, dear? You look so beautiful—let me know if anything comes up, OK? You're an angel.

Before saying goodbye, she gives my shoulders a squeeze, a way of saying thank you, I suppose. She looks me in the eye without blinking and grimaces, as if she wanted to smile with her nose. The skin of her face remains absolutely static, which adds a disquieting, not to say frightening, touch to her look, the way a doll that's suddenly come to life would terrify the children. Her irreproachable breath invades my nostrils, I'm feeling ill, but I manage to hold her gaze.

Delia accompanies me down to the first floor again, exhaling in a heavy whisper, *such a catastrophe,* more to herself than to me. I can see her in the mirror delicately biting a hangnail on the thumb of the hand in which she's holding the keys with the Hard Rock Cafe Cancún key ring. A pink convertible.

Horses

Not entirely aware of what I'm doing I head toward the polo field. There's no one around, neither out here nor in the city itself. I take advantage of the desolation, the approaching holidays, to look in at the racetrack just across the street. The horses raise a dusty wake that remains in the air even after they've vanished, the dirt track so dry you can taste it on your teeth, as if biting into burlap. How long is it since you rode a horse? you asked me at our final dinner, at that place with the pianist and the red lighting. I said that's a bit of an aristocratic question, isn't it? I've never ridden on anything more impressive than a pony, and you said that everyone gets on a horse at some point, that I take satisfaction in acting like I'm poor.

I'm looking at the track through the gates, and beyond it there's nothing. The afternoon light crowns the earth in a golden haze, the glow of Hollywood movies during the Great Depression, the glow of Shirley Temple's curly locks. I know that there's a merry-go-round on the other side of the parking lot. Things in my head are spinning around like teacups. I got to tell you that ideas were spinning around in my head like teacups. After that you stopped responding.

Before leaving I lean against the gate with my back to the racetrack and smoke a cigarette, replaying the music of memory, Xuxa, the condiment dispensers at Wendy's, my mother in her dark glasses and white sweater, nut-brown lipstick.

Going up the Juan B. Justo overpass, the vertigo of the mannequins on top of Montagne. I don't know why but this is where I always imagine you meeting Violeta, the scenario I invariably construct. You were shopping for jackets and she told you the yellow one looked nice on you. The timeline gets a little fuzzy; after all, I found out only when the whole thing was already well underway, practically from the newspapers. Why do I imagine the two of you here, in the shadow of the overpass, in a shop that may not even exist? Strange notion, but that's how I picture it. To me, the idea of meeting people outside of family circles or established social structures always seemed weird. But that's just me, one of my "little quirks."

I wouldn't exactly say the night came upon me unawares but it arrived a bit sooner than I expected. I didn't have the energy to cook anything elaborate so I whisked two egg whites for a low-calorie omelet. Watching the egg swell up in the pan to the consistency of a cloud, fatigue came over me, a fatigue so profound I felt I could fall asleep where I stood, narcoleptic fantasies.

Yohaku no bi

There's an interior design magazine on the kitchen table. I flip through it as I think about what I'm going to do with the rest of the day. I like magazines, but since I try to think logically and not with my heart I reflexively dismiss them as worthless. Though I do love the irresistible way they combine information of different densities, the photographs one can absorb without really paying attention. It relaxes me.

As a girl I dreamed of being an architect, because the architects I knew lived in beautiful houses like the ones in magazines. What I wanted most of all was a house with lots of different kinds of rooms, with secret hiding places and plenty of glass. It's why I started peeling off the wallpaper in my bedroom when my mother wasn't watching: I wanted to have those smooth white walls.

One of the main aesthetic ideals informing the design of Japanese gardens is called *yohaku no bi,* which means "the beauty of the void." According to this principle the void defines the useful part of things: A glass is not the crystal but the emptiness that it surrounds.

Containers in this house that are visible at a casual glance: vases (two), yogurt jars with snap-on lids (plenty), jam jars with screw-on lids (idem), Tupperware (various sizes), water glasses, wineglasses, bottles, ashtrays, guitar case.

Now let's see if I can express this clearly: Things are missing in a way that isn't obvious at first. Some books, removed almost at random, leave gaps in the shelves of the studio library; in the bathroom there's not a single personal hygiene product, as if it had been emptied before a move. The things that are missing are missing in very particular ways, there's a certain inconsistency to their absences. The one that disturbs me most is the old mirror in the hallway, which had always been there, from the time your grandparents were still alive. Only a ghostly reminder on the old pink wallpaper that you never wanted to change. Without the mirror this isn't the house I knew so well. Something truly vital is missing.

There are two kittens and they're only a few days old, fifteen, to be precise. They don't need to be fed yet and it's best not even to get too close to them since Materia is being so protective. They made them a little bed out of towels and other soft odds and ends to keep them warm.

I'm not so good at caring; not so bad either, I just don't stand out one way or the other. There are people who have a special talent for it, though, and they've always inspired my admiration. People with a kind of radar that detects the risks in a situation and consequences not yet visible to others, a sixth sense for possibility. For example, the mother of my grammar school classmate Valeria always had the right-size Tupperware and the perfect portions of everything, a Band-Aid, an extra change of clothes, a sweatshirt, an awareness of other people's allergies, a gift for navigating a heterogeneous group with the warmhearted English efficiency of a Mary Poppins.

Once we were asked to bring some eggshells to school to make an organic sculpture in art class, so she pierced the shells of two raw eggs with a pin and patiently drained out the yolk and albumin. Valeria arrived with two perfectly hollow white eggs that I envied so much I had to hold back my tears as I squeezed a transparent bag of slippery orange and white fragments, hardly even washed because my mother said they were obviously intended to make a mess; they'd asked for trash and how could you do any better than this?

Mental Zilch

Last night someone gave me a crystal and now I'm floating. The cats are asleep, the gentle rise and fall of their flanks as they breathe melds with the rhythm of the peaceful afternoon, a light breeze puffs out the sheets they left hanging on the patio. They've been dry for some time but I'm only here to observe: the fields, the sea, the music.

The first time I took drugs we were in Mar del Plata. Like most of my first times this was also with you. You said that ecstasy would help me relax, that it was mental zilch; you were right. To come down from it, you told me with medical authority, I had to focus on simple movements, that it was a very physical drug. I can see us tossing damp sand into the air to watch it fall like rain, I can see us balancing on a highway divider at dawn pretending we're walking a tightrope, I can see us going back on the bus with our hands entwined and resting limp between us, eyes fixed on the pink sky above the side of the road.

It's hard for me to leave a place and just as hard to return. When I'm at home I don't want to go anywhere but when I'm out I never want to go back. That's why I said yes, even though it was getting late, even though I knew it meant I wouldn't get any sleep. It was a big crystal and unusually bitter but once it was on my tongue it dissolved right away and dance, dance, dance.

At some point it rained, the sun instantly came back out and over the side of the armchair I can see a ridiculous sliver of limpid sky, as blue as detergent. Moebius woke up and brought me his plush stuffed mouse. Although he's a father now he's still a kitten and all he wants to do is play. My body's in neutral; nevertheless I throw the mouse, whom we prefer not to give a name so as not to have to feel pity for it, as far as I can. To christen is to form a bond, to open the door to empathy.

I root through the drawers, desperately looking for some electrical tape. My cable has gotten frayed, if I don't fix it the battery's going to die and right now it's my only way of communicating. I was sure your laptop would be here, that's why I didn't even think of bringing mine, but it's not and I don't think you have it with you, either; they made it clear that you'd be completely cut off for now.

Why did you keep it, this horrible little notebook that I made for you? I found it while I was looking for the tape. Of all the things there were, why would you have kept this one in particular? A pathetic bit of craft of no value whatsoever, or maybe some kind of value, but a confusing one. I'm completely annoyed that among all the things that could have represented us you chose this cheap little paperback notebook adorned with my pompous, pseudosnobbish collage.

Definitely something I wasn't expecting and it made me feel tremendously uneasy, as if this utterly trivial thing could symbolize our entire life together. I open it. It invades my body, first a clenching in my stomach, the feeling that you can see what I'm doing, discovering your secret, violating the wooden privacy of the closed drawers. Like a mother's gaze on the back of your neck, X-rays that cut off your circulation until your hair falls out. Like my mother looking in through the half-open door the day that Barbie had sex with Ken for the first time. And what if everything in it is meant for me? What if it was all staged so that I would happen upon it? "We're about to explode; I'd hate to think of you ever reading this." A setup contrived to make me feel rejected, even in my own imagination.

I have a vague recollection, deliberately repressed: I was embarrassed and I still am that I was pretending to be an artist when we met. The girls who'd won you over were truly different, they all had the makings of painters, or singers, they all felt like potential threats, they all had something better to offer than I did. I suspect that I never actually gave it to you, that you stole it; I have no recollection of the moment of putting it in your hands, nor of the sentence, divided in the middle, that I glued over the spine: "without fear" on the bottom and "into the silence" on top.

And now I'm going to sleep in your bed, like that night I came to your place in a taxi I couldn't pay for. I phoned you over and over until you finally woke up; you came to the door in your pajamas and I kissed you, one of those kinds of kisses that hurt. We were kissing, I was on top of you, and suddenly you looked me in the eye: What is it with you? What do you want? you said. This was before the notebook, I'm sure of that. We didn't have cats yet. You didn't know how to take care of anything either.

Spatial Intelligence

Among other odd items Violeta left her Coco Mademoiselle and quite a bit of clothing. I couldn't resist going through it all, trying everything on. I'm a girl alone in her mother's room, making a mess of her lipstick and shuffling across the floor in her enormous high heels. I make excuses for myself: I forgot to bring my perfume with me.

I'll be busy all day on a ridiculous outing involving my cousin, the one who's a little slow, and a trip to La Plata. I wanted to show some solidarity for once when I agreed to accompany him, not foreseeing that I wouldn't sleep a wink last night. At times I feel presences, a peculiar energy, the certainty that something is going to happen, a break-in perhaps, someone coming in through the roof. Sometimes I'll get up to check the burners on the stove, the image of dying in an explosion, being blown through the air, terrifies me.

We're cruising down the highway listening to some harmless electronic music, music that's never made anyone cry and will probably vanish completely in the future, like the skin of dinosaurs. I imagine grabbing the wheel, getting off at the beach exit, and heading for the surf, but first I have to hear Manal. All I can think about in the summer is the ocean, and by any criterion, beaches or rock formations, I choose Argentina. You tried to make me feel bad about loving its coarse sand, cold water, and violent wind, but to no avail. I'll never be one of those girls who say they're going to "Uruguay" when we all know perfectly well that they mean Punta del Este and that Punta del Este is not Uruguay but an alien, dystopian place whose inhabitants can wear only white.

We take some guarana (he says it's like speed); I instinctively jerk my head to keep from falling asleep. My slow cousin seems to take pity on me, he hands me an impossible silver magic-cube puzzle that I'm supposed to reconfigure into a prism. I feel like a child who has to be constantly entertained to keep it from having a meltdown. Over and over I try to solve it, I vacillate between feeling like a genius and feeling like an idiot; I have no spatial intelligence.

It's unexpectedly cold in La Plata; we have a craft beer and when I begin to shiver an Adidas sports jacket magically appears over my shoulders. I feel a sadness come over me—though I sometimes confuse sadness with the weather—the kind that reminds me of gathering up kindling at summer camp to make a fire. The little twigs don't actually mean anything, it's all just symbolic, an exercise in group solidarity, most of it won't even light.

Materia

Night, and the house is full of blood and news, a precarious, third world sort of terror. I gather up the glass, make a careful package of it, put sugar on the wounds I can reach, clean up with a rag, as if you can wipe up blood the same way as the remnants of a meal. Materia keeps her eyes fixed on me, crouched as if ready to attack again. Her distrust defeats me, being scared of her makes me feel like I've failed completely.

Lucas texts me a message that your mother has written to him as well and that he's worried. I answer that everything's going to be fine although I really don't know. To be honest, with the house so dark and shards of glass stuck in my hands I don't really know what I'm saying. In fact, I'm insecure too, wavering. I want the cat to love me again and that's the only thing I care about right now. I want to feel like I've succeeded at something, however modest. I want the house, your things, to return to their static and well-lit order. He asks what I think about your situation. What do I think? I don't know, when it comes to that I've got a blind spot.

That the cat I gave you attacked me is probably one big metaphor for something I don't understand because the pain and the urgency of putting everything back in its place isn't letting me poetically relate the immediate facts to a life full of broken glass. She went crazy in a way that I couldn't anticipate, that's how accidents work.

A demon had latched onto my leg with the force of a thousand lightning bolts; I knew I couldn't pull her off, that that would tear open a piece of my flesh. It's incredible the things one knows with a weird certainty when faced with a real crisis, an uncanny prudence tied to desperation. At some point she clamped down harder and when I wrenched my body in pain I put my arm through the living room door.

I got away with only superficial wounds, but hands bleed profusely. At the hospital they told me it was a miracle I didn't sever any veins. The idea that they could have found me dead in my underwear on your living room floor flashes sensationalistic headlines through my mind: Girl with No Job or Future Bleeds to Death in House of Psychotic Ex Following Mysterious Incident with Hypermaternal Cat.

When I left the emergency room I decided to go to a party, as I was, all bandaged up. I didn't want to face Materia again right away or what still has to be cleaned up, and the pain had already subsided. Sometimes just hearing a doctor's voice is enough to anesthetize me. I danced to every song and came back when it was light enough that I wouldn't be afraid to walk down the corridor; the dark corridor terrifies me.

Unnatural

It's your birthday, but the visiting restrictions are still in place and no exceptions until things settle down. I slept as much as I could, the heat woke me up. You're definitely right, it's unbearable upstairs without the air-conditioning. It's not that I wanted to contradict you, it's because I have the impression that air-conditioning dries out my skin and throat. At my mother's house air-conditioning was strictly prohibited, she considered it dangerous, unnatural.

I swept up again; my cousin, rather limited but handy, will come tomorrow to replace the glass I broke. It seems implausible to me that one body can pass through another and destroy it. I finished cleaning a few isolated droplets of blood and the sugar crystals, which had attracted a battalion of ants and flies in the shape of a heart. I mopped the floor, I'm still unable to open the washing machine and I don't want to ask for help. I'm worried about the kittens but I can't get too close because I don't want to invade the mother's space, especially not after what happened.

I made a list of everything I need to get through the next month or however long it takes to do whatever it is I'm doing here. Every second that passes I'm more uncertain what it is that I'm actually taking care of. It's overwhelming to open my datebook; I brought it but left it in my backpack and haven't touched it since I arrived. There are specific things I should be dealing with, paperwork, lawyers, that I seem to want to forget. I distract myself concocting suspicions, exigencies, plausible scenarios.

At some point in the afternoon the light was just captivating and I took a picture of Moebius stretched out on the bed asleep. The back of a sleeping animal is the picture of improvisation; I want that golden sunlight forever, I want to be that cozy slumbering creature.

While I was cooking the kittens started moving around the house. They take a few clumsy steps and go back into their den. I don't want to look at them; from the sound they're like pompoms hitting the floor. I pretend it's not a big deal that Materia is still threatening me; she tracks me as if warning me not to be so foolish as to get between her and her offspring, circles me like a lioness.

Good Fortune

She cried in her sleep. The moaning made me nauseous, guttural spasms that seemed closer to physical pain than to despair. She cried so much it actually deformed her face. I never got used to her new features, it wasn't her, the hollow eyes always dissolved in a haze of alcohol. It wasn't her.

She broke crystal glasses and replaced them only to break them again. Slivers of glass got stuck in the soles of my feet more than once before I understood that I'd always have to wear shoes at home. She broke glasses and cried while listening to baroque music; little by little she let go of everything that had any sort of a clear message, of words. She also stopped reading.

One night I was awakened by smoke coming from the kitchen. The pink candles that she'd been lighting to improve her fortunes in love had set her favorite tablecloth on fire and the table was about to be engulfed as well. My first impulse was to smother it with a dishcloth. It was a small fire.

My mother almost burned down the house, I told you the next day. You chose not to take me seriously, to treat me like a naughty pet just trying to get a reaction from its owner. That night my mother almost burned down the house with the two of us inside.

The Spindle

I woke up freezing and with a terrible sore throat. I always get sick when it starts to get warm, I run counter to the logic of the seasons. I slept some more. While taking a shower, I thought about what I could bring you as a gift if you're ever allowed to have visitors, my breathing becoming more difficult by the second. Maybe it's a panic attack; yeah, it's definitely mental, I repeat to myself, but suddenly my throat clamps shut like a metal door. I cough, I cry, involuntary reactions. I bend at the waist and try to do the emptying-the-head and opening-the-lungs exercises I learned in online yoga classes.

Edema of the glottis. A shot of pure intramuscular adrenaline. With it the immediate sensation of the larynx expanding, recovering its natural pliancy. And the tension in my neck abated right away, but I was still scared, relaxed and on edge at the same time. It took a while to get myself to the hospital because I refused to show up in the emergency room twice in a single week. A sort of superego blockage related to shame, like that stretch when I just couldn't bring myself to deal with bureaucratic stuff. I imagined that everyone else had a clear idea of how to manage things and that they'd make fun of my incompetence.

The cable of my cellphone charger finally broke. I hope the medication makes me sleep; if not, the nothingness may be unbearable. My cousin didn't show up and what's left of the glass in the door has a frightening edge to it, a sharp and deadly stalactite.

I thought about pulling it out, premonition of the wound.

Like the spindle of Sleeping Beauty's spinning wheel that mesmerizes her until she lets herself be pricked on purpose I let it pierce me. In the story, the one we all know, she falls asleep and the prince has to fight against dragons and writhing vines; the kiss awakens her from death.

It's not like I really want to hurt myself, it was just an imaginative reflex that invoked the scenario, but it does give me pause. It's certainly fascinating what it reveals, though I could never just surrender myself to injury that way, however attractive I find the idea of someone risking everything to save me.

Sorceress

Turns out I'm allergic, probably to feathers. Your pillows gave me the idea, the feeling; or it's to fur. There are too many cats, I should vacuum the place thoroughly and keep it clean. And try not to break anything else.

It was by chance that I started collecting holy cards. The other day I went into a bookstore and came across a Jesus inside a book dedicated "To María de los Remedios, may you never be lacking in love or in faith." It's not about making fun of religion, but I see something similar to tarot cards in them so I take them as signs, as messages. It's their aesthetic; they've got a medieval vibe.

I'm constantly performing rituals to keep myself calm. I cook industrial quantities of food that end up in the trash. I imagine you in a gray space with a vacant stare and my body is crawling with worms from my belly to my throat; they want to get out.

I look at the dagger around my neck; against the black dress it makes me look like some kind of caricature, a creature of the night, existentialist, esoteric, a dark sorceress collecting herbs out on the heath, and you're an alchemist; burned together at the stake during the Inquisition.

A little murmur interrupts me at my preparations. The twins are at the door, trying not to make any noise in that way that children try, in vain, to be stealthy. It's a witch making potions, they whisper. I listen to them as I cut the onions. I raise my eyes from the counter to avoid tearing up and there I see it, a black cast-iron cauldron in the pot rack above my head. In a single bound they rush off when my big round eye surprises them at the keyhole spying on me and I hear them vanishing into the distance.

The Stain

I still can't sleep more than an hour or two straight. I thought I might be able to sleep more soundly with the corticoids but nothing so far. I really feel like smoking, or maybe I don't feel like smoking any more than usual but since I'm not allowed the urge is more intense. It would be a good time to give it up again but I don't even want to risk trying so I won't have to face the further frustration of failure if I can't. I'm ugly, I have bad skin, and my hair's falling out again. All I do is look at myself, but I don't do anything to make it change. I wish that Google could solve my problems. I look up how to make your cheeks thinner. I grimace, make a bunny face in the mirror.

The thing that's killing us is the elections. What happens to all our optimistic projection if we make the wrong choice? It settles into the fissures, temporarily sustaining a structure we therefore cannot see is precarious, like tile covering a rotted wall that will crumble under the force of a single sharp blow.

There are swollen tiles like that in the house and other problems too, wooden latches on the verge of disintegrating, faucets that won't quite shut off, but I'm trying not to take out my frustration on anything; enough with the self-fulfilling prophecies.

I don't know what the future holds despite so much planning: I Ching, Lacan, astrology, tarot, crystals, homeopathy. I'd like to graduate soon, but it's going slowly, like everything at this school; I've reached the chewing gum stage, stretched to the max, with a backlog of final exams I'll never be able to pass. I watched *El estudiante* and thought maybe I should get involved in politics, an idealistic spirit pulled me in, a Marxist vortex, fear of what the coming years hold in store, capital flight, gutted institutions. I'm well aware of what you think about all that.

I should concentrate on fixing myself instead of trying to hold onto what they're going to take away from us anyway, sort things out on a personal level, buy a car, get a partner, etc. Get out of limbo, untangle things. My mother used to tell me that sometimes life unravels all of a sudden, that she was lost, all tangled up, and one day everything suddenly unraveled. What I never understood about the knot metaphor is why you would want to untie it. Wouldn't that just make you feel completely unmoored?

Now I'm worried because of the dark corridor so I try not to go in or out very often; it's a challenge, a game I play with myself. I wouldn't be able to bear the confinement without the sun, it's the light that helps me stay indoors.

A lot of not being able these days, a lot of reading to overcome not being able to act, a lot of not talking to anyone, a voice thick from not using it, from saying only a quick hello to the fat neighbor who for some reason is always at his door; I see him when I go out to the drugstore or the little Chinese market, my only excursions.

Whenever I need something, I keep hoping until it's hopeless that someone else will deal with it for me; when that doesn't work, I proceed slowly, protecting myself against theft or accidents with a mantra that goes *keep me safe, keep me safe*. Sometimes I tell you everything that's going on in my mind, I also talk to the cats.

Ping-pong in my head, to light up or not to light up a cigarette that I know is going to be painful. You'd encourage me to do it. Our disagreements were always over that sort of thing, with whether and up to what point to prioritize safety over experience.

I stayed awake, I have to take my medicine at eight and was afraid I'd oversleep. Moebius was yowling loudly, he was frightened and I couldn't tell where the sounds were coming from. Honestly, the stupidity of your animal amazes me: He was stranded on the narrow edge of the dividing wall and didn't know how to get back down. I had to go up onto the terrace in a nightgown—Violeta's, of course, you know that I don't wear them—and show him how to do it. Apparently he just needed moral support because he found his way immediately once I started urging him to come. Now, in the kitchen, he's bumping into everything, he bangs his head on the underside of the counter and bats his metal bowl from side to side, making it screech as it scrapes over the tile floor. I don't have the will even to try to understand what's up with him, what he's trying to communicate.

He heard me typing and came over with his filthy mouse and put it on the bed; it made me gag. I have to take my medication in an hour and can't let myself doze off. He wants to play; I don't. We're not in sync with each other. The staircase is too steep, the rooftop is dirty, years of accumulated filth. When I walked along the edge as if I were an animal with a keen sense of balance myself I remembered the night I fell from a second-floor balcony and the only thing that happened was a little cut on my back. Again the premonition of an accident: without a phone, the neighbors all asleep, my head bursting against the ground like a watermelon.

That time I fell down the stairs Juan took off my dress and patched me up in the bathroom. Before I passed out, which confirmed that I needed to go to the hospital, I apologized to him. Why? he asked. I woke up a few seconds later; I never answered. The triage staff at the Hospital Italiano were friendly, they cleaned me up, bandaged the wound, asked me about substances I might have taken, possible pregnancy. They did a CAT scan because of the blackout, took X-rays to rule out broken ribs. There was a little cut on my back that didn't even need stitches, though it did leave a scar. I had to throw away the dress, I couldn't get rid of the stain.

Compromised Hope

I'm still without a phone and therefore without an alarm clock. I had yogurt and fruit for breakfast at a ridiculous hour; I want to be thin again, but the healthy kind of thin. I have to go sign some papers with my aunt downtown, endless inheritance issues. I also have to go to my department to resolve something with my student records. I never had possession of the master copy and now it's apparently a problem, or that's at least what some threatening emails that I get every year tell me, but today they actually grilled me about it; sudden respect for the institution. I have to get the medical check ups I should have gotten seven years ago when we started college. There are vaccinations I never got, vaccinations I blew off on a whim, Hepatitis B and another one. Everyone got them when we were sixteen, but I didn't want to and nobody objected, like when I wanted to remove my braces early and you helped me take them out with a tweezers.

I'm spending more time thinking about solving things than actually solving them, I try to put together a schedule, and once I do it seems impossible to keep it. Inability to compromise with reality is part of my problem, I can only do extremes, all or nothing.

A passion to take control, control over something, it doesn't matter what; it's the urge to take the reins that gets me out of the house. First I take money out of the double-decker-bus-shaped jar, I have to buy a charger, charge the phone, catch up on things. I fantasize that I have thousands of messages, surely Anita at least must have called to make some plans.

Strange freedom. I await your emotional telegrams as if they're part of a duty from which I can't escape and don't know if I want to; any hope I have is compromised because I don't know what might happen later on: wait for you to put yourself back together, keep you company, and then what? It's all so vague.

There's a guy I've been seeing, but we haven't talked since Saturday. Actually, we exchanged texts yesterday, though just a few. He's sort of addicted to dating in a general sense, I have nothing to do with it, I mean it's not like he specifically wants to be my boyfriend, mine. What I do notice is that he puts a supernatural energy into it: He's constantly proposing things to do, he's curious about my opinions, and he likes everything that has to do with me, he feels like every bit of my personality is "so me." He says "Oh, that's so you." He showed me some songs he wrote, he's a musician. I liked them. I think he expected something more specific in return; I told him I'm not exactly known for my musical knowledge or sense of rhythm. We'll see if it manages to hold together like this, our asymmetrical desire; in this case it's not like one has more and the other less, but that we have different expectations, expectations made of different materials that don't quite mesh, but they don't conflict with each other, either. I'll see how it goes, I don't want to force any changes, keeping still may also be an answer.

Speed

This morning I talked to Juan until the sun shone bright over the metal canopy of the terrace. We finished what was left of my Marlboros and started in on some Parisiennes I found in the kitchen drawer, which did away with the last vestiges of my voice. The conversation got more and more minute, examining every detail, recalling over and over again everything we knew, the last things we all did together as a group, the signs. I rummaged through the story for some hint of a forewarning, my issue with trusting history, with believing that we're pure chain reactions, that we can find a logic behind it, an invisible thread connecting and uniting everything.

I fell asleep at seven in the morning and got up a few hours later, mostly because I needed to feel like I could accomplish something. I made a mental list: Gustavo (I owe him for a session)—mineral water (buy plenty)—bank (is it already closed? what time is it?)—read that stack of books—read one book—read something later on tonight.

When I go somewhere, I have to leave the house with time to spare because I'm so slow and always get distracted. It's been like this forever: the last one to get off the bus after a trip, dragging the maroon sweatshirt; the last one to get a piece of the coveted *chocotorta* at birthday parties, the one with no candy to show after the piñata bursts, who gathers the useless plastic combs and develops a peculiar fondness for confetti. I always wondered whether my mother dwelt so lovingly on the unique tempo with which I did things because she linked it to a certain sensitivity, or if, as a matter of fact, it was proof that her daughter was an imbecile. In any case, instead of struggling against my nature, I try to leave myself enough time, even more than enough, to be able to walk if I have to: I don't have a great relationship with buses, either.

If I'm going to arrive late somewhere a sense of disequilibrium comes over me, a voice inside tells me it's better to stop trying than to fail; my transportation options seem unclear, everything speeds up, time, ideas, my heartbeat: he's going to hate me if I cancel, but if I tell him I haven't left yet he'll hate me more, I can't tell him, but I have to; if I take a cab I still won't get there in time, well, calm down, dress yourself slowly, you're in a hurry; take a cab, no, I won't get there anyway, OK, cancel, but what's my excuse? And so on.

I skipped therapy and sat down on the curb for a few minutes to watch what was going on instead. The thrumming of the wind made me think of high school, the last days of the final semester, using our residual sick days to sunbathe in the backyard, eating those thin chicken, tomato, and cheese sandwiches we'd buy at Esther's kiosk, the moment when we no longer had a curfew and could walk unaccompanied back and forth between our houses until we were hungry or tired.

I need the regimen of a serious job, to have a routine, get up every day with a goal in mind, take the same subway, have a cubicle and paste up pictures of the Caribbean on the wall, perform mechanical tasks at the computer, wear blouses, long for the weekend, get a regular paycheck, go to the gym, maybe adopt a dog. I ate a piece of cheese and looked for free meditation courses online. I drank some water and coffee and wept, with both hands over my eyes, like a maiden.

Where the Wild Things Are

I'm blowing smoke rings, the years I didn't smoke are out the window, as if that never happened; I've surrendered to aesthetic vice. And it's not just the going up in smoke, the neighbors' noise is exhausting, they're like beasts, they howl. The ceiling is opening up, like in that story I must have told you a thousand times, although I don't have much confidence that you'd remember. One night Max misbehaves and his mother sends him to bed without dinner, he finds himself in a forest and becomes king of the monsters. With no mother, no rules, nobody sending me to bed, I'm like him, adrift, trying to dominate or control something that's real only in my imagination—the tidal pull of your influence.

Heartbeats

I finally watched *Heartbeats* to the end for the first time; I had always struggled, maybe because it's the kind of film that everyone assumes that I'd like and I prefer to thwart expectations. It's a story of hysteria. A completely bourgeois and aestheticized romantic triangle. So affected, so contrived, that in the end it seemed even more realistic to me. The use of slow motion was painful. Painful like meeting the perfect new girlfriend of an ex you still care about and always will, like when we ate with Violeta for the first time, on my birthday, "Cool" by Gwen Stefani. Everything is imaginary, love is always imaginary, you remember we once said that? That love is a soliloquy. Your soliloquy, my turn never came.

The boyfriend I have these days is like the one in the movie: I give him gifts, I have my hair done. I stage a whole performance of love, the sweet messages, for nothing. It doesn't even manage to distract me until you reappear and I have the glue again to reconnect the scattered pieces; it all feels like a performance, everything slightly staged, for someone who isn't even watching.

Cockroaches

I encountered the first cockroach of the season, they're so exuberant that it's hard to understand why we find them so unpleasant, they're practically an ode to life with how plump and juicy they are, how disgusting. I couldn't bring myself to kill her, so I took her in a rag and brought her outside. I've never been so brave.

I could hear the crash a block ahead, on Billinghurst. We were on our way to buy some nails to secure the glass in the doorframe. The guy with his ankle sticking out, the fluorescent white of the bone. A handful of nails is two pesos. He told me: They have to straighten out the leg, don't look. But I did look just a little bit.

Back on the avenue I took a picture of the window of a shop that sells hourglasses, I looked at plastic fabric that's used to make tablecloths. I cook a chicken, for a few seconds I'm back on my axis. When I walked out of the subway downtown it started pouring rain; I bought a cheap, transparent umbrella. I rode back in a cab looking out at the wet asphalt and lights splashing on its surface. What's the life of every person who lives on this street like? I imagine some plausible scenarios using houses I've been inside of. Collages using the houses I've lived in, the little tricks of living in each of them. The trick of this one: never to lock the door so as not to be stuck outside in the corridor that has no light and is full of the corpses of toys.

Like an Engine

I'm not pregnant. I was astonished by my own blood, I had nobody to talk to. Whom could I tell that I thought I was pregnant and that I'm not anymore? Would my mother have helped me understand my body? Would my mother have suddenly started up like a dormant engine knowing that I was losing her potential grandchild?

A blood clot hanging from a grayish alien that resembles a lizard, intense abdominal pain. I stand in front of my lost thing, I don't dare to refer to it any other way; nevertheless, my eyes tear up. I swear to pretend that it never happened, that I didn't go off on a fantasy tangent imagining a rotund, inconvenient child to nurture with love, using what I know as my model, the cat with her kittens. He starts walking and I have to go running behind him so he doesn't bang into something. In the scenarios with my baby you're not there. I'm alone with him and I'm glowing, I paint his name in acrylic on the door to his room and I'm wearing friendly colors, dark sky-blue and white.

I'm waiting for news from you, I'm the embodiment of a wartime postcard, an anxious woman waiting for news or the confirmation of a death. It's ridiculous the number of bridges you have to build just to communicate in this Internet era. I smoke to kill the time I don't know how to use. The cigarette gives me the same displeasure as always. The smoke strikes the palate and, immediately, the lack again. To fill yourself with smoke is to fill yourself with a contradiction, an insubstantial substance. Killing yourself slowly, the way cowards do.

I picked up a backpack of clothing from home and also brought some creams and wipes and tampons. I got myself to hang the clothes in the closet and considered that a triumph. It was a gesture to see if I can somehow get back into a routine if I no longer have the excuse that I can't find anything. Always having your bags packed is proof of not being settled anywhere. They took up a shelf and four hangers, as if I care that the things don't get wrinkled. I bought a cleansing brush to remove impurities from my pores, did some beauty rituals. It came with a white headband. I plucked my eyebrows and drank warm water with lemon.

Reflections while washing my face. What's the connection between water and thought? I won't even get into the scorpion invasion. You have to check the sheets before you go to bed, and even then they can still sneak in anywhere. Now there's all that stuff about post-truth. I wrote down a reminder to research it, especially for when I run out of topics of conversation at parties. I'm so bored lately you have no idea.

A Flash of Lightning

I tried on my mother's wedding dress. Yesterday, when I went to get more clothing. It's undamaged, time hasn't inflicted a single blemish on it. The thought had never crossed my mind before. It's a simple dress, everything was simple, a modest civil ceremony and a small meal at tables decorated with jasmine bouquets. I always imagined it would be too big for me, maybe because I always felt small, as if my imagination was inhibited by a sense that the dress was for grown-up people who got married. I'm the same age my mother was when she got married. I also have her hair color and her eyes and her bowlegged knees. I considered calling my father, I thought about it for a millisecond before ruling it out, like when it occurs to me to become a vegetarian, a flash of lightning that instantly vanishes.

Prickers

When I said I love you, you replied "same here." Interminable days in captivity. I wanted to tell you I'm feeling it too, but the whole lie of hijacking a real victim's tragedy is among the most despicable scams of our generation. You didn't ask about the house, just watched the videos I sent. Wouldn't it be nice to have a kitten soup? you say. Yes, somehow they're tantalizing, everything to do with love is delicious, a feast we devour, and maybe vomit back up again. You want to just drop everything and go home, you say, as if you're on vacation. It feels like a dry joke, summoning only a single "ha" that gets caught in my throat like an unsatisfying cough.

My hands are full of tiny prickers that stuck me when I tried to reposition the unidentified plant near the cat litter. Am I selfish to think about us, or am I deceiving myself that I care only about you and your progress? We'll be able to talk better when I'm taking fewer pills, you say. I'm scared that you're not going to be yourself. I remove them one by one with a pair of tweezers. I have to examine my fingertips over and over because there's always another one that I hadn't noticed. Could my body absorb one of them, engulf it, keep it forever, make it part of me? Could I be the beginning of a new human-plant hybrid? I'd deploy them when I got angry, jab you when you're on the verge of having an attack, not to hurt you but to diffuse the tension and make you relax.

Now we're talking without middlemen. Like babies starting to walk we have to take it slowly, learning a new language to reconnect. It's midnight, a day has passed. There's something in knowing that it's you telling me "I'm fine," even though *I'm fine* is an empty phrase we say even when we're falling apart, that it's you sending me your emotional telegrams and not someone else, something that both relieves and terrifies me. The way you're using words is like a zombie, it's you and it's not you at the same time. Or maybe you never made sense and I just wasn't able to see it before.

Floating

I read in some book that our days aren't individuals but soldiers. Which is true when we're not anticipating anything definite, that there's no meaningful way of measuring time if we have no milestones or hopes by which to mark it. I mark mine by portents and dreams and by concocting absurd countdowns. You're the one in isolation, but I feel like I'm inside of a Gesell Chamber.

I dreamed that I stole my sister's first husband and that my cousin was hosting a barbecue in his room. The grill was made of hangers, and items of clothing were mixed in with the food. To get back you had to wait for a bus on one side of the coastal railway station. I was eating *alfajores* with my girlfriends when I saw the guy I'm dating, and I told him: "I don't like it that you're always wearing that same shirt." And I started to cry. He didn't move; he didn't react at all, just stood there.

He was playing somewhere tonight and I overslept; I told him it had been a complicated day and he didn't reply. He's stopped asking about you and about how I am, how I'm coping; he already knows everything. It's basically over. The gig near the Abasto, and everything in that neighborhood reminds me of you, the Peruvian restaurants, the theaters. I can't have a boyfriend that isn't you. I don't have the energy to keep up the charade.

Materia moved her nest while I was sleeping. Now the two kittens sleep behind the armchair on the window side. Last night I danced alone until dawn. *El amor después del amor* and

Virus all night long with can after can of beer, resisting the urge to drink anything stronger. Getting drunk slowly is the best way in the summer. In the winter it's different, liquors and chocolates make sense, you need layers, but when it's hot you have to let yourself just drift away. The pain is intense and relentless and sleeping helps relieve it. I'm in a state that feels like floating, just my head out of the water and making circles with my arms near the surface, like the old women at the swimming pool.

You said I have a hippie side but that our hippie sides are different. That if it were only up to those sides of us we'd never have crossed paths in a million years. You also said that my idea of tragedy doesn't come from the Greeks but from American movies, and not even the already limited satisfactions of film festival fodder, with its pastel aesthetic, but of the genuinely bad ones. Stories about families conflicted over excessive consumption at Christmastime. And with a moral to boot. It struck me as passive-aggressive, but, still, you had a point, so I let it go. As usual, we were both convinced that what we think of each other is the truer perspective.

Luminous

My mother was cultivated in a way that's hard to quite put your finger on. This affected me, but only in the way that things that are always there affect one, coloring your reality, like the kind of blinds that won't open past a certain predetermined limit. She knew about a lot of things, always watching television documentaries, but earlier in life, from what I can gather, she'd been an avid reader. And every now and then she'd divulge one of the staggering truths she'd been storing up. One morning, handing over my breakfast as if she were delivering the mail, she blurted out, "Sunlight is a natural antidepressant," a lit cigarette dangling from her lower lip. I'm obsessed with getting sunlight, and I attribute my trouble falling asleep to the fact that I'm always anxious for it to be daytime again.

At seven o'clock in the morning the world is absolutely luminous, objects have clear boundaries, everything is perfectly defined against its background, and that entails a certain perspective. It feels like one is truly capable of doing something, nothing transcendent perhaps, but at least full of vigor. And then everything falls apart the moment the light begins to disperse. What was clear and distinct has now become a problem. What had been an obvious possibility is now a quandary. I can see only the plates piled up in the sink, smudges on the windows, objects getting in the way of other objects, and everything ends up conveying the sense of an irrecoverable loss.

Janet Leigh

I'm captivated by the way the kittens are growing, hours on the cold floor observing how they learn to use the strength of their paws. I have a fleeting Augustinian illumination, as if I could feel God in my chest as I inhaled, an intuition of the true miracle of life. I'm not going to turn into an antiabortion nut or anything, my limits are clear enough, but the proximity of death can make you sensitive to the texture of what you normally take for granted.

I remember that Violeta still hasn't come to pick up her things, which sets off a strange echo in my head, a whispering that intensifies until it commandeers most of my inner voice. Just now I wanted to use her aloe vera conditioner and when I tried to open it it slid out of my hands in a triple somersault. Spilled cream invisible on the white surface of the bathtub, premonition of slipping. The scene ends with the shower curtain torn from its rings, confluence of blood and water streaming toward the drain.

An amazing trans singing Christmas carols; I'm sitting on the floor doing backup. About twenty of us walk to a party afterward. Dizziness. They ask me how're you doing? Fine, thanks for asking. They ask me what I'd like to drink? The questions. Dancing. I stay until dawn because I can't bear to walk through that pitch-black hallway. A Bach adagio's playing in the cab, a sly moon and a single star punctuate the soft fluorescent blue of the magic hour turned upside down.

Trivial Pursuit

I do the wash by hand. The murky water, acidic smell, the density of the sodden clothing hanging there. I still can't open the washing machine, I don't even want to know what's in it. I do switch it on every once in a while, like keeping the muscles of someone in a coma active so they won't atrophy. I want to apprehend, to understand the world, by touch; I massage soap into hardened stains that are as dark as holes.

I forgot to take off my rings, they leave marks on my fingers. It's gotten cold, my voice is almost gone. To *how's it going,* you say you know now. I ask what, and you say you were wrong. Leaning on the bar, I quickly guzzle a beer and order another one.

Back at the house with my friends and the second bottle of rum this week. Their eyes are like platters gaping at me in astonishment, nothing gets me drunk. We play Trivial Pursuit and I know the answers only to the questions someone else has been asked. I lose every game, but they show solidarity, try to convince me that it doesn't imply anything about my intelligence or define who I am in any way. It was all sunrise and friendship and background music and alcohol without drugs until I said that you were OK, that I'd been able to talk to you, and Juan replied, honestly, I couldn't give a fuck.

Which slices through the dust-speckled air like a saber. Rips through my clothing. Anime. I can't even ask him to leave, I'm feeling constrained this morning with the kittens batting at the zippers on my boots. If I ever cared it was only because of you, he says, and it sounds like a line that Adrián

Suar would say trying to sound tough in one of his movies. You know perfectly well what I think about that sick bastard—another lunge. I don't even know why we're here, why you look after him. More slashing. With his little girlfriend curled up in the crook of his arm staring at the dregs of her red wine, Juan keeps on thrusting. And we keep playing the game; it's my turn.

Vicious Yoga

In my dreams, I don't smoke. You appear as a composite of yourself and Juan, you turning into a cat, you in two places at once. Construction sites abandoned in the eighties, the building in which a friend of my father's had an advertising agency in the nineties. Persistent congestion in my throat makes me think I've got cancer. An old lady's cold that won't go away. I have nothing left to eat but I still can't bring myself to move.

I'm trying to determine my limits, it's a form of extreme therapy. Provoking your body until it finally reacts, as if to a vicious brand of yoga, introducing or denying it anything as if it were all part of an experiment. The cotton mouth. The fear of opening the fridge. The same old fear of walking out the door. The paralysis of shopper's indecision. Days go by in bed. The distinctive light of each passing hour, the graduated shades of anguish.

I never know whether it's early or late, I don't do anything. I wait for the telegrams and imagine the apocalypse the new government's ushering in: looting, political persecution, Gotham City, forced to burn our own books. I'm living outside of time. Your mom wrote to me inquiring after the plants and the cats. How are you, she asked me, how are you and the babies, the plants, everything OK? You'd have to be an idiot to let a ficus die.

Champagne in Las Violetas and afterward a thousand beers at the Chinese bar next to the bookshop. I doubt that

I actually like beer, I think I'm only trying to shut down the demands of corporeality. To crush something out.

Bumper Cars

We're holed up in the kitchen snorting coke from an antique teaspoon. Not so much to hide as to safeguard our conversation. Whiskey on ice after wine after beer. This stretch of the night transpires on a loop, gazing at the spoon, lighting the cigarette, golden whiskey slipping across silverly ice cubes. In the end you'll get pregnant and he won't say no.

At what moment do we stop being girls? Like the simile of the ship whose parts are replaced one by one until nothing of the original is left. To what extent are we ourselves at all? We're all wearing short skirts, our legs are brushing against each other's as we improvise a twister choreography to all get inside at the same time. One pees, the other puts on mascara, another pokes around in her bag looking for the right lipstick. You can tell a lot about someone by which brand of cosmetics they use. You know if their family has a beach house, a country estate, or both. Could you detect a suicidal mother, an actress aunt, and a nouveau riche father from mine? Something I've always taken care to ensure is that it's unclear where I come from.

I see the lighters go by, the glasses, the magazine hairstyles, the essays, their sources, the undeserved preferments. I stay on the margins of the conversation so as not to seem rude. One has to come to terms with the fact that it's unnecessary for everyone to talk when we all think more or less the same things; if one person expresses the whole idea that's enough. They talk about an artist who openly supports Cambiemos, they say that that's the reason why she got a Fulbright for her doctorate at NYU. I spot Lucas on the other side of the terrace, turning his back on the discussion or, more accurately, absent from it entirely.

How are you going to come across? That's what he's worried about, whether you're going to behave normally. It's not the time to make a joke but if there's one thing I can't connect you with it's normality. I accept his offer of a ride home but when we get into the car I can see that he's at least as drunk as I am. I don't say anything, you don't judge. I pray the entire trip that his reflexes won't let him down. I can see the car smashed to pieces, my mother alive and I'm the one dying first.

Rice Paper

A woman feels pain for the first time in her life as she's closing in on forty. She was born with a genetic aberration that inhibits her ability to experience physical pain. People with this anomaly often don't feel hunger or fatigue; a British girl got the nickname "the Bionic Girl" because she was afflicted with the same condition. She was run over by a car and was so relaxed that she survived without a single broken bone because her body didn't resist the impact.

With my throat numb from cocaine, that story caught my eye. They've ruled out that your problem is chemical, repeating the same verdict in various ways: There was no toxin involved, it wasn't a result of intoxication, it's a structural issue, inevitable. Even trying to find a way to make it seem logical, everything about your situation seems nonsensical to me, maybe even amounting to some kind of cover-up.

When the girl felt pain for the first time she tried to reverse her condition, to figure out a way to avoid passing it on to the children she wanted to have. It's very dangerous not to feel pain, you can burn yourself, lose parts of your body, you don't have appropriate reactions. They gave you back your phone because if the problem isn't chemical it poses no "danger."

It took me a while to remember that I still had leftovers from afternoon tea the day before. My Aunt Ana insisted on taking me to one of those pompous banquets at Las Violetas and of course we didn't manage to eat everything. I'd love to be like Ana if only she weren't so obsessed with her youth. But you can't have everything. I wish she had children so it wouldn't be so bleak thinking that it's just us on this side of the family. I wonder what it would feel like to be from one of those families that go on trips together as a gang.

I eat a few pieces of cheese and some olives, I drink what's left of the flat Inca Kola, inside of me everything's churning. I remember those months when I never had a problem eating, I didn't drink or smoke, my skin was beautiful and I felt good, morally superior even.

The orange cat tried to eat his parents' food. They still aren't able to chew. I bought them the wrong kind of food so I had to soften it with water. In theory it's still a few days before they're supposed to be weaned and start eating solid food but they seem to grow quickly, or maybe their appetite's growing more quickly than they are.

I haven't taken a shower in a couple of days, now I'm trying to convince myself that this could be good for me, another one of my idiosyncratic therapies. Tomorrow I'm going to do a thorough cleaning up and I'm definitely going to start studying. I always promise myself that it will be tomorrow.

My nose hurts. I feel threatened by the dampness of the walls and the accruing pile of dirty clothing. The dust on things that forms a film, one on top of the other on top of the other. I'm terrified of the neighbors, I imagine them conspiring to rob me while I'm out, breaking in by force and smashing things to pieces. I stay still and try not to make any noise, it's the only way I can think of to protect myself. I don't know what caused my inertia in the first place, if I'm inherently unmotivated or if my problem is chemical. I hope the new day will restore my will. You suggested we talk in a few days, that you were too pilled up, and I don't know what it was about that phrase, so simple and straightforward, that threw me off-balance, my whole body feels like rice paper.

Creature

If I go out at night I can't come back until dawn. Fear of the dark. But I try to get myself out of the house as much as possible. And this is the one who was never afraid of anything, who used to be so self-assured. I don't know where she got to. Now I'm afraid that they'll rape me, or rob me, that the neighbors will talk about me.

I got Juan to accompany me back here on foot, I invited him to join me for a glass of rum. At some point he got the wrong idea and threw himself at me while I was reading him some articles on the computer. Not only did it not turn me on, it positively terrified me. I told him I couldn't, and he asked if it was because of you. He told me that I have to get over us and he played the motherhood card to upset me. I'd given him the ammunition, I told him my period was late and about my fantasy—my therapist had said it was a fantasy because I'm always late. He told me that I'm not going to be the mother of your children, that you always said you're not going to have children and that in the end you'll knock up some random woman who wants to tie you down and that'll be that. I told him it has nothing to do with being a mother. He started kissing me on the neck and tried to open my pants, which absolutely revolted me, though I'm the one who ended up apologizing to him.

It's useless to try to reconcile the differences, we're a different person at night. The darkness blurs our edges. The feeling of having a Mr. Hyde, as you described it a long time ago. I tried to dig deeper, but that's all you were willing to give, just a category. The empty template of your thought.

When I got up I went to eat at a place on Honduras that has air-conditioning. A scorching sun, kissing, violating everything. I go to the mall, it seems like a holiday. I try on dresses. I like a white one and tell the saleswoman that if it looks good on me I'll take it as a sign that I should get married. She says my boyfriend will love it; I agree and say, yes, he's very sweet. I lie to salespeople and service workers all the time. I once told a guy from Movistar that I was a dancer with the permanent company of the Teatro Colón ballet, and he believed me.

I cleaned the floor and now I can go barefoot. It's been a long time since I saw my feet, and I'm disgusted by them. It's the only part of my body that's exactly like my father's. Someone told me that when I was a kid, I think it was my sister. I always forget that I have a sister.

I didn't feel like cooking, so I thawed some empanadas that were in the freezer. The other day I read a story about an old woman who prepared meals in advance for her husband to eat after she was dead. What an odd idea to interfere with the natural deterioration of things, to preserve them for an after. Walt Disney waiting in some cryogenic chamber to be revived and create more characters with the new technologies of the present, his future. The empanadas made me feel sick. Eating them I imagined they could be made of just about anything, they could be poisoned or full of hair collected for some weird ritual. I had to throw them away.

The orange cat brought me a huge cockroach as a trophy and left it in the middle of the living room. I follow the contour of its thorax, its legs are still pliant. But I can't touch it, a force field prevents me from picking it up and getting rid of it. It's unbearable the desolation that something so small can instill. I try again, but I'm still confounded, if a little closer now. The sensation of holding it and really feeling its lightness, its consistency, descends upon me. That's exactly what I can't bear, how much a thing that almost doesn't exist at all can weigh me down.

It's the constellation of ideas around the cockroach, not the bug itself. I believe in instant karma; a while ago I killed a bug and it felt like an accomplishment, I even dared to call myself brave again. Now the bodies of dead cockroaches torment me, stare me down with their absurdly long antennae. Sickeningly perfect, like every creature.

Identity

They've started eating but I have to pay particular attention while they do because their parents want to steal their food; it's more nutritious, designed for growth, and it's clearly much tastier. I try to train them to let the kittens eat in peace, but it's pointless. I have to physically insert myself to keep them away, just hoping that the babies will gobble it down quickly. But my technique does improve a bit from time to time.

When they finish eating, they start to play, their way of showing that they've had enough. I suspect that there's an instinctive component to being siblings, and these are clearly brothers; they pull each other's tails and chase and hug each other. That never happened with me with my sister because we have different mothers, although I'm not in a position to assert as scientific fact that that's the reason. I call them darlings, and beauties. My heart softens when they're around, as if nothing could be wrong in a world in which there are baby kittens. One of them is flesh-colored, almost pink, and that's the one I'd want to keep. Should I give him a name that's on the intellectual side? The first name of a jazz singer? I've always felt a bit envious of people who manage to give their pets spectacular names that don't feel at all contrived. Am I trying to suggest that our names affect who we are?

The sun gave me the energy to go to the market and I bought a chicken that I carved up like a pro. Broiled, with lemon. I cut a tomato into quarters, spun some lettuce. The huge cockroach remains in its place; I'm expecting it to get deader and deader, drier, or rather that it disappears on its own, that they'll hide it, or eat it.

Aspen Radio

Whenever I look at the clock the numbers repeat themselves or else the time is a palindrome. I try to discover a sign, a message, that mania for finding meaning in what troubles us. I'm worried about the future, about time, and, above all, if there's a way to know what I'm supposed to be doing. I don't know what I am. I try to detect the presage of a vocation in the games I liked to play as a child. I think about starting a clothing business, for example, because as a girl I liked to dress up. I'm lacking the drive that turns desire into action; I think they call it will.

I made the most of these unexpected "holidays" and rented my place to some French women, bicycle included. I recommended bars to try and things to do around the city, the euros fatten up the (modest) bank account that supports me. I don't know what my mom would have wanted me to do with the money. It's not much but maybe I could have invested it instead of feeding the inertia of the precarious *petite bourgeois* that I've turned out to be. I could buy a cab and drive around Buenos Aires, it would be a good outlet on sleepless nights. Aspen Radio playing, no doubt, meeting people I'd never see again, listening to their stories, gathering up shards of the world and piecing it back together again.

Adulthood isn't going to announce itself, my analyst says it's time. This limbo of drifting along on my inheritance and the odd freelance job isn't working. It's true that I won't run out of money, but in order not to be crushed by life I have to find a purpose. Money's a disease.

I peruse the cascade of names and events on Facebook. A lot of people exist conclusively: They're in swimming pools, they're drinking orange drinks, red ones. Thereby reaffirming their lifestyle. They have a partner, they graduate, they drive cars. Sometimes I feel like we're alone, that everything else is just a set, that there's really no one left to know out there whom we don't already know. Maybe even we don't exist, not your mother, not Violeta, not Lucas, not Juan. Even your illness. Even my memory. This voice isn't an I but just a mark in the sand, a ripple on the water.

Bodies

Today I was almost hit by a motorcycle while crossing the street, I'd been watching a man struggle with an impossible number of balloons. How many do you think it would take to levitate a person, a person of average weight? Girls are showing off their golden legs. I'm gray and haven't shaved, I'm wearing shorts anyway. Among the bodies, I try to locate one similar to mine to figure out if I'm really unpleasant looking. But there's no way, each one is so different that I get lost in the minutiae of comparison.

The heat is all-encompassing. The outdoors itself feels heated. I heard on the radio that there was a yellow alert. I don't stop drinking water just in case, I set an alarm to remind myself. They're trying to make it look like it's nothing serious, that it's just a rough patch that we'll get through, but tension is thick in the air, I feel the shattered assumptions. I've been believing for so long that others are taking charge that I have a sudden feeling of guilt about the state of affairs. I could have been doing more.

It feels like my materiality is in question, as if it's being emptied of meaning. I'm an apparition, a floating mind. I'm taken aback by my image in the mirror. Like the time I took up dance again and couldn't follow the steps because I didn't recognize myself. I fell down and I was so embarrassed that I had to run out of the room. We were dancing to "Beat It" and I felt as if the shapelessness of my body reflected the very essence of everything that advertising told me was wrong or comical about it.

The Same Stone

I ended up out on the sidewalk with two anachronistic punks, straight out of 1978. My head was lolling, my cigarettes had gotten wet. I'd tried to bring in an uncovered glass of rum, stowed vertically in my purse, and it spilled almost immediately. The liquor in that club is terrible and there are no flasks at your house. Why do I always end up going where everyone else we know is going, no matter how awful the plan? Tripping on the same stone over and over again. I find it difficult to maintain my facade when somebody asks about you, as if I know that any response I can come up with would be a lie.

I'm not ruling out the possibility that I might be developing some kind of paranoid delusion but I feel like people get bored with me. Maybe it's just that my ability to pay attention is compromised and nobody likes being with someone who seems to drift off of the planet in the middle of a conversation. Worlds are always opening up, subterranean worlds of ideas and thickets of images that prevent me from registering the details of the here and now.

I can't remember conversations unless something suddenly shines, a sparkle of contrast, a comment so incongruous that it becomes a pearl or a flare. Probably why the only thing from that night still pulsing in my memory is a friend of Juan's who bizarrely compared you to Matías Alé. Cut to a few minutes later sitting on the sidewalk with the punks till I can collect my thoughts. I come back to the house, eat some bread, put my cellphone in a bowl of rice. The next day didn't exist.

Flashes of lipstick passing from hand to hand, poisoned compliments, advice that no one asked for. The ecosystem of the party: seduction for sport, not knowing when it's time to leave.

Intuition

An orangutan's reaction to a magic trick makes the news in the States. The trick consists of making a ball disappear in a Styrofoam cup. It's completely rudimentary, like when adults pretend they've pulled off our nose with their fingers. The orangutan roars with laughter every time, and I'm saddened by the feeling that they're making fun of him. Who's above whom and why? At this point in the soirée, it seems ridiculous to have actually believed that my nose was being pulled off by someone's hand, almost impossible. Although I have to concede that it could be the resolute maturity of my current frame of mind that's preventing me from reconnecting with my own innocence.

After watching the video a couple of times, the twinkle in the ape's eyes sparks a revelation: He believes it, and he's having fun. Believing in magic transcends the inimical binary. Why not be more naive? Why do we always denigrate the intuitive? Care should be intuitive. Not hurting oneself or others should be intuitive, not putting oneself above any other being.

I've started biting the skin again on the sides of my fingertips until they're raw. My hair and eyelashes are falling out in clumps because I haven't taken off my mascara in three days. I'm a bucket, something that needs to be filled, but it's as if I had no bottom. If I had to think of myself as one particular thing I was always a bucket, or maybe no more than a saucepan.

To retake control at least to some modest extent I decided to repair the seams of a cheap skirt that had come undone.

I did the sewing with the skirt still on, like the doll in *The Nightmare Before Christmas*. The doll is enslaved to an evil scientist who's intent on possessing her. To get away from him, some nights Sally throws herself down from the loft, whereupon she bursts into a thousand pieces on the floor below. Since she's a rag doll she can stitch herself back together, requiring only her hand to do it.

Anemone

The towel hanging on the doorknob looks like a ghost, the popular image of a ghost. Sometimes, you ask me not to tell anyone anything. I nod and wonder exactly what secret it is that I'm keeping. Or more than just the secret, from whom am I keeping it? Whom are we protecting you from or whom are we protecting, and why? I speak in the plural although in this case it's only me.

Suddenly, the idea of stepping barefoot on a cockroach doesn't seem so serious, as long as you didn't know. The problem is to kill knowingly; I can't crush something if I'm fully attuned to its vitality, of what that means. That's why I'm immobilized in the face of bugs, no matter how unpleasant they are. I'm unable to assert myself over them, not sure it's fair to attack them. Even when they've already been half killed by the cats, for example, I freeze and can't be the one who cuts the last thread that binds them to my reality. I need them to die apart from any decision coming from me.

It was overcast all day, indecisive rain. The quality of the light renders the stains on the ceiling visible. The white light of cloudy days reveals the flaws that the golden sun tends to glaze over. It's a harder light, or our vision is harder when we're waiting for rain without realizing that we're waiting, the rain that always circles back around without becoming anything more than a few transient sprinkles.

I broke into tears at the supermarket. Something overwhelmed me, the price of things. I've gotten used to buying only what I can carry by myself. No more than four bags, and I'm always running out of supplies. My plan is to cleanse myself with fruit and hydration. Cleanliness starting from within.

I left half a ripe pink grapefruit covered in plastic wrap in the fridge. I was fascinated by the compression of the plastic on its surface keeping its freshness intact. Slapped on the plate it looks like a vital organ or an obscure saltwater animal that's been wrenched from its environment. An animal so strange that it looks like a plant, an anemone. Very marine, one that can be found only by diving, which glows in the darkness at the bottom of the sea.

Haptic Memory

Open-mouthed, staring at the ceiling while having my gums scraped, I receive a call from an unidentified number. I'm very sensitive to such interventions in my body and, given the tears, I have to start brushing better. I thought it was your mom, that thing about protecting her identity. It wasn't, it was a telemarketer from the bank calling to offer me another credit card. I didn't accept because I didn't want to think, everything concerning banks raising doubts because I distrust them on principle; I'm a child of keeping money under the mattress, opposed to speculation. I asked them to call back later; they haven't and I still haven't done the thinking.

Fucking makes me sad, though it's not instantaneous. The cat got jealous and ran away because I came home with a guy. Today someone called me to come pick him up at a house down the street, the pianist's house; he wasn't hurt, just scared. He got stressed out by the traffic noises and he scratched my throat as I was bringing him home. I look like a battered woman.

I don't want to sleep here now, I feel like it left a lingering film in the air. I should change the sheets. Last night, as I was trying to concentrate on sex, I ran my hand down the back of his neck and my haptic memory kicked in, suddenly I wasn't there anymore. Just like during conversations at parties, sometimes I'm just not there anymore, not here. In my mind I recount the plots of movies, I make to-do lists, I fake orgasms.

I went back to the supermarket. I can't help but stare at the aisle of toys. It's the colors; nowadays there are all different kinds of dolls, not just blond, there are dark ones too, as if made just for me. He insisted that we see each other again, he told me to call him if I'm feeling lonely.

Looking over your books he said that reading Salinger is a cliché. But maybe that's not why I don't want to see him again, it's the issue of building something from the ground up that's oppressive, I don't want to have to get to know anyone from scratch. Familiarity is oppressive, the process of getting to know each other, getting closer. I already decided long ago that my personal universe is unpresentable.

I talked to your mom about the cat's escape, she asked me if Violeta had already come to pick up her things; I said no, that it makes sense that she doesn't want to come back. I forget about the implicit no-judgment rule when I talk to her. She asked me if the air-conditioning was working properly, if everything was in order with the neighbors. Nothing about you.

On the Other Side of the Rainbow

Last night the storm. I wasn't aware that there were leaks, I ignored them. I took the opportunity to open the windows so I could sleep with a breeze the first night that the heat index wasn't above ninety-five. But it was difficult anyway because the cats were crying and I wasn't used to the noise from the ceiling. At times, it seemed as if the house was going to come unmoored and fly away, like in *The Wizard of Oz*. Toto, I have a feeling we're not in Kansas anymore. The heat subsided a little; it's going to rain again, they've been saying so for days. Finally something happened just the way they predicted it.

I watch the news passing through social media, the infinite scroll. I decide to fix the closet door. I was OK with the damage but the idea of starting a project calms me down. And I'm terrified by a particular vision: The cats knock it down while playing and die beneath it, crushed to death. I'm also going to change the burned-out light bulbs.

My watch fills up the silence, it's got an assertive second hand, so much so that back then you made me put it in a drawer at bedtime because it "unfocused" you as you tried to fall asleep. I don't know whether the superstition still persists that in the moment just before sleep we can simultaneously inhabit otherwise disparate contiguous worlds.

Today I didn't leave the house at all, which implies its own peculiar state of consciousness. The cats are noisy, I don't know if they're chasing bugs or if they're chasing each other; I hear them running around and bumping into things.

Photosynthesis

The plants died on me. I tried to save the one with the pink flowers, but I didn't get to it in time. They got too much sun and perhaps I was a little unreliable. Which is a euphemism for completely negligent.

I didn't sleep all night. I smoked like a chimney, an expression my mother used to use. I changed the sheets and I only fell asleep at six in the morning. At nine the cats started calling for me to feed them.

A few days ago I decided not to take the final exam. I didn't say anything to my classmates. I have more time now, but I don't know what I want it for. I tossed and turned in bed.

You say that we're going to be friends forever, that everything's alright, reassuring me because you know that I'm teetering on the edge and didn't want to talk to you because I'm not OK. I know that you'll explain later, I still intuit things as well. I tell you I've been using drugs and you say that you noticed. I tell you that I knew you had. You say that everything's going to be alright. I tell you the kittens' mother has been talking to me.

I went to a party on a rooftop terrace, there are rooftop parties all the time in December. I ran into Juan, who was there with a friend. We took four taxis, did the whole circuit: bar, pool, disco, his place.

He liked my dress, we stole a bottle of wine and kissed in the elevator of Juan's house on the way out. It was already morning and we passed through the flower markets, the melancholy of seeing people already about their work when you haven't even gone to sleep yet. I had hiccups most of the night. We arrived here around nine in the morning. This time the sex wasn't depressing, I even managed to come. You always thought it was funny that sometimes when I come I get caught up in a fit of laughter. That's what happened today.

I won't be seeing him again. Incompatibilities. Kids, he does a lot of coke, I don't understand how he supports himself. He didn't stay over because of the light. He can't understand how I can sleep with the blinds up. The sun was never a problem for me.

Offering

There's a dismembered bird in the middle of the kitchen, feathers all over the place. Not much blood, but some, and guts: The kittens tried to eat it, and I had to rush to get to therapy. You told me it's the greatest show of love for them to hunt their prey and bring it home as an offering. I couldn't find the keys and I was running late, there were little pieces of body and I swept them up, trying not to break down. The afterglow of orgasm didn't last very long.

I went out with the trash bag in my hand and put it in the container. I took a cab. During the session I told him that I realized that I'm not indifferent as to who fills this space. Welcome to the world of decisions. I don't need drugs; no, you clearly don't. No one needs them, well, of course there are people who need them, but you don't.

I'm going to my aunt's to spend the afternoon. There are bird parts I didn't have time to clean up and it's bothering me. I ask if she could come with me later on, at least to keep me company while I vacuum.

She needs to go to the bank and tells me to stay and rest, that I seem down and that when she gets back she'll help me finish cleaning up the muck and feathers. Cats in houses do that, she says, it's not malicious. I'm afraid that they'll kill me in my sleep.

The case is over and I receive a little money, it's been so long that the actual sum has become irrelevant. The bundles of cash fell apart and now it's scattered all over the bed. The bills feel meaningless. I count them, looking for a mistake. I put forty thousand in one drawer and almost ten in another, keeping out a thousand for immediate expenses. I have to give you back the eight hundred pesos that I took out of your emergency fund.

I ran out of mineral water and the tap water, which you never let me drink, tastes just like at my house, nothing weird about it. Or maybe mine's contaminated as well.

The Enemy

At some point, I couldn't stand the cats anymore, they're so demanding; I think they miss you, or maybe they miss her, I can't imagine you being patient with them. I can't stand the house either, it gets dirty way too fast. I thought about it yesterday while vacuuming the feathers, that a house with so many animals and so many openings is too much work.

It looks like you'll be coming back soon, the treatment's working. Gradually resume activities. I still haven't heard anything from Violeta, I don't think she's coming. I can't wait for you to come back so I can leave. I love knowing that you're OK but what I love most is the idea of getting out of here. The house talks to me and silences me. I see little tragedies in everything about it: sharp edges, things that work poorly, stains and the remnants of a situation of which I don't want to know the details.

The unexpected sex made me remember something about myself. It was beautiful to come with somebody else, to give instructions, connect with each other's bodies. Ever since the accident every time I tried to think about fucking my ears felt clogged. I couldn't even touch myself, I couldn't get to the point of feeling the urge or I got distracted in the middle by some incongruous thought. My bodily pleasure had dissolved, something seemed wrong. As if I felt watched. Schoolgirl morals.

I still have tender feelings for the little ones, their bodies are warm and they're unexpectedly light. It's the parents who make me crazy with their noise and their demands.

I don't have any dry panties so for hours I've been walking around in a towel. Everyone's asleep and I can only hear the noise of the water dripping in the bathroom. They lifted the currency restrictions and nothing depresses me more than sudden and unnecessary changes. Truth be told it's not very realistic or inclusive to set a cap of two million a day. I think about inequality in general terms. But who am I to get upset about inequalities? A sinister layer on top of reality.

It's cooled down a bit but the sky's been gray for days and it rains from time to time, heavy rain, and then it stops. Wind and then a little sun again. It feels like being at the shore without the sea. The wooden staircase, the bed on the mezzanine.

I started packing my stuff. Although it's not for sure that you're about to come back I don't want to forget anything. The cats read my mind, today Materia sank her teeth into me again. I was leaving and, when I nudged her with my foot to keep her inside, she latched onto my leg, this time the right one, looking like a malevolent little gremlin.

I remained calm. I poured rum over the wound: You have no rubbing alcohol, no hydrogen peroxide, no gauze, nothing that would help heal anything. I had to improvise a bandage from the "Hello Kitty" Band-Aids that I only bought so I could get some change. What do you mean that I want to be part of something I'm never going to have access to? What kind of access are you talking about? Or rather, to what?

I can't stand the cat hair on my clothing anymore, I can't stand them wanting to be loved and then hurting me, offering me dead things. I don't want the dead things. But what do you mean by that? The same feeling as when you said that thing about the enemy; what does it mean? You already know what my priorities are, you say, that you don't need to listen to me. You're a monster.

Stray Bullets

I called off the idea of fixing things. As far as I'm concerned they can break it all; I see that the two babies have climbed up the cables and I think: What do I know? Last night a bag flew in through the window. An invasion of what not even Hollywood can persuade me to find beautiful. I say that's enough to the cat and he whimpers, he understands. Enough already. It feels as if the inside of my body were dirty, like when you haven't brushed your teeth.

Now they go at full speed, they already have complete confidence in their limbs, they run around everywhere; I don't want to pick them up much, I'm afraid they'll ruin my new clothes.

All the towels are full of hair, they managed to get into the closet and I only noticed it when I was drying myself. I feel surrounded by the sheer force of defeat. Trying to find an acceptable towel the loose door came down on my foot. I choose a white one even though I know that I'll soil it with the blood from the wound, which gushes out again after the shower. I didn't go and get a tetanus booster, the day got away from me, and now I'm imagining gangrene.

The French women have gone, leaving behind a fluffy aroma in my apartment, like an infant smelling of milk. They left an open bottle of wine and some good cheeses, some imported beauty products. I'm going to use it all.

Today I was surprised by a call from my father inviting me to spend Christmas with him. He imagines it must be difficult, he says, since it's the first without my mother. The second, I correct him, but without hostility. I've never had strong feelings regarding the holidays, neither good nor bad.

The only picturesque memory I have of Christmas, my mental model of it, is from 1994. The last year they were together they bought a tree that reached the ceiling, decorated with frosted gold and red balls. Mom made Scottish tartan and golden bows, after that she never bothered with another piece of ribbon in her life as far as I can recall. Later on, kids always asked if I was Jewish and I started saying yes; it felt like a clever solution. Anyway, that Christmas was nice, I got a Baby Flo, whose bottom got chapped and you had to put a cream on it. My sister got clothes from John L. Cook's and a ticket to see Emanuel Ortega.

That summer we went to San Bernardo for the whole three months. Mom bought me lots of T-shirts. I started to sense that there was something strange in the compulsiveness of it, every day a couple of T-shirts, nothing else. Some, luckily, were big and they lasted a long time. When we came back from that triplex where all of our acquaintances had come to spend at least a couple of days getting tanned or playing cards in the cabana by the ocean my father's stuff was gone and Mom didn't get out of bed for a year. That's how it started.

I tell myself I'll be OK, if Ana doesn't go on vacation maybe I'll get together with her, even though she's more into popping a pill and falling asleep until the madness of the holidays subsides. She's thankful for not having dogs so she doesn't have to comfort them when the fireworks begin. My dad asks me, for the first time, if I'm OK. I remember the days when he'd be worried about stray bullets.

Natural Disaster

I want to go back to normal. Whatever it is, I want to go back. Yes, I'm terrified of facing reality, the feeling that I'm doing everything wrong anyway, as if giving up on myself at this particular moment is just a way of tripping over everything that wasn't working out between us all over again. I had a life, a house, a personality, damaged perhaps, or "overly susceptible to influence," but it was mine. I want to go back to a state that felt logical, at least within my own sphere of possibility. I feel like I've been dyed: Though the contours and fibers are still me, I'm not easy to recognize, and I miss my mom. Like when you spend more than one night at a sleepover. Like when you go on a long trip and need to return to the comfort of your own life no matter how routine and complicated it may be. Here and now: the potential for tragedy, the thin air, as if a natural disaster were in the offing, threatening me from the first meow. It's all a blade poised to cut me to pieces. It's like a boa taking my measure so as to swallow me whole, the furtive calculation of a silent ambush.

Like the boy in the plastic bubble, I don't know what it is, but there's a force that won't let me break through to what is clearly within my reach. As long as you love me, I'm OK, you say. And nothing about me. I don't need love.

Another bloodstain, this time while cleaning places I'm sure you didn't even realize existed. They exist. What did you do? I can't assemble it all in my mind. A hank of hair as if pulled out by force, long hair. The pieces are falling, but not into place, into chaos. The cat hugs me, or I hug him and I feel it's reciprocal, I can't stop crying.

Nightmares with my mom. She melds into you, not in a romantic sense, you're the same person. I get up kicking at the air. I even unplug the fridge to perfect the silence. I fold in on myself, I want to be small, tiny, I want to feel my specific confines, to be a definitive being. There's nothing left to clean, no clues remain, I scrubbed every surface with a scouring pad.

Coils

I didn't sleep in Billinghurst last night. I called him. I needed to feel the strength of a real, available, present body. I hadn't come back home since the French women left and I needed to know that something of mine was still waiting for me. He looked through my records while I rearranged the space, so much mine and so patently not nobody's, to my taste. Suicide's not a common death, people look at you differently. You could be just a girl until a death like that touches you. Then you're the person everyone's afraid to talk to about certain things. Parents can't be mentioned, even simple happiness. You know, *know* that people avoid showing you their good fortune. At times that hurts more than the death itself, because the silence is obtrusive. It's so clumsy the way people navigate others' tragedies. I don't think I've had a relaxed conversation since my mother died, and that certainly wasn't my choice.

Francisco knows almost nothing about me, which is why it works so well. He doesn't need to be cautious. He thinks it was something normal, like cancer. Whatever normal might be, I can hear you saying.

I slept so deeply that I lost all sense of time, I was embarrassed by the drool stains on my pillowcase when we woke up, but he acted like it was nothing; he's an easygoing guy.

My house felt truly welcoming, my own things occupying my own space, a sense of belonging I can't remember ever having had. He watched me doing normal stuff, washing dishes, lighting mosquito coils.

Hawaiian Tropic

Although I'm not especially fond of buying things I feel secure in a shopping mall. I'm not a person who plans out what she'll need and then allocates a budget. I'm a sporadic shopper and I mostly go to the mall when I want to disconnect or have fun being someone else. Ana wanted to buy gifts, for me and for herself, some "things for us to remember by." Girls are buying white linen outfits for the summer in José Ignacio, an unparalleled sadness suffuses me. I try to crack my neck and I feel all pixelated. There was a time when I had occasional and transient spasms. At some point the discomfort intensified and became constant. As if my body had been structurally modified to become uncomfortable to me. A nuisance I ended up accepting as the way things are.

You can get used to anything. I'd like to find an exception, but you can accommodate yourself to any stimulus that's systematically present, the way people who live on busy streets stop hearing the sounds of the traffic.

I wish I could wear bright colors with dignity, that way I could at least hide the mourning. I've always dressed in black, in dark blue, it didn't seem to attract anyone's notice, but since I became a poster child for tragedy people suddenly see me as gaunt, pale, in need of beta-carotene.

Tournerie

A person's profession can be read in their hands. And it's precisely by her hands that we know that Ana will always be a ballerina. Before my mom got sick the dream we all shared was that I would follow in her footsteps and even go to France like her. The Paris of my memory is a place of such plenitude and happiness that I've never been able to return.

She selects everything she consumes with the precision of the great theaters, heading toward objects with the confidence of an usher leading patrons through the dark, never stopping to consider anything that isn't worthy of her attention and going directly to the item that's calling her, her self-assurance in stark contrast with the diminutive woman whose growth seems to have been interrupted halfway along, like the foot of a geisha.

The same things people hate about Ana are what fascinate them. She already talked about the toxicity of dairy products in the nineties, she uses pink Himalayan salt, pronounces the names of meals in their original languages, and sleeps wearing a mask. Her spine is so straight that she always seems to be looking at you from a superior position, as if standing on a bench, even though she is, in truth, quite small.

At the age of fourteen she debuted as a soloist at the Teatro Colón, at sixteen she entered its permanent company through a competition, and at eighteen she starred in *La Sylphide* alongside Maximiliano Guerra. She had already begun traveling at that point, touring with a French company; as her domestic options accordingly narrowed her international stature grew, and she ended up remaining abroad.

Her gradual but definitive departure coincided with the definitive but gradual departure of my mother. One day my mother informed me that I had to decide between getting an education and doing dance, because dancers are all stupid, and she pulled me out of classes. There are parts of my body that were tied to the dance and sometimes I still envision myself spinning like a top. That's when, thinking about that fantastic other possible life, I feel like I'm betraying her.

The first time I took a plane I traveled alone. The stewardesses had to board me and at Charles de Gaulle Ana was waiting for me with her bun. She cooked, I liked that. I spent three months in France, maybe a bit more. My mother would refer to that time as "the year you spent in France." I found out later that it wasn't that she was confused but that she liked to confound others. The truth is I never missed a year of school. The truth is I had to go and stay with Ana because I didn't have anyone else. It always made me feel guilty having gone to such a beautiful place at such a difficult time. My mother made me feel, depending on the day and her whim, as if it had been something she'd arranged for me purely as a gift or that, since it had occurred as a result of her misfortune, I'd taken advantage of it because I'm such a despot. Even today it fills me with shame, or I suppose it's really guilt, that I speak French so well.

Bruise

I went back home today. Earlier in the morning I stopped by your house, Francisco accompanied me. The kittens wove between his legs and I just set out their food, and then some more. It's my job, I told him, and he said, how sweet. If it were just that, it really would be sweet, but every day I feel that it's more like a cage I've gotten myself into and then swallowed the key.

At home with the birds I awaken to a different type of clarity. I'm relearning the sounds of the block, imprinting new possibilities on the day.

I dreamed I was seeing a different ophthalmologist, it was someone I knew, but possibly not a doctor. Examining the bones in my face he realized that my prescriptions had always been a little off and that that could be causing me confusion. After that I take a family trip, it's a big family that includes the doctor's, or it's something he's telling me and I imagine myself being there too. We go to New York in the winter and when I get back I go to a swimming pool, I have two babies that look like dolls, I'm talking about the poetry of adolescents.

I started emptying Mom's place. I don't know how the devaluation will affect real estate transactions, I have to find that out. Anyway, I thought about selling the house and buying a different one, changing neighborhoods. It scares me to imagine being happy, having a nicer house, as if I were profiting in some way. I'll divide up the clothing, some to give away, some to sell, the rest, the things I like most, I'm going to keep for the future. I don't want to handle them for very long because

I'll end up keeping them all. I talked to my dad, he told me he could help me think. We've never talked so much.

Draped across Mom's bed I see the filaments of light streaming in from the yard, the green reflection of the vine. An unfamiliar energy takes hold of me, I feel the urge to do things, to cook, to drive, to go out to the countryside, to the mountains, swimming in icy lakes, having fun.

I marvel at the evolution of my wound. The bruise passes through a whole spectrum of colors and the scab where the cat bit me shrinks slowly into nonexistence. It makes me feel strong to have these wounded legs, like the wild girls of my childhood, climbing up trees as I ached with fear and desire from below.

My dad picks me up, he's got a new car again. He says he still has the Honda truck if I want to use it, it's in perfect condition. Big cars make me feel insecure, out of proportion, constantly thinking I'm going to crash. We could never agree on this; my father wants me to drive, but he wants me to do it his way and in the car that he chooses for me. I've had my license since I was seventeen, and today, at almost thirty, I'm the shame of the relatives still living in Nordelta, me a resolute pedestrian and all of them fearless helmsmen.

We barely talk, I look at my phone. A car reduced to half its size in an accident; no one survives that, he says. The remains are in there, as if pinioned in a trash compressor. He moved a few years ago, his ex-wife kept the house and he bought a "small" apartment; I'm surprised to see some pictures of me in the study. Lunch is fine, we don't talk much; he understands.

He brings up the subject of you. He was always a little . . . a little . . . I don't know, a little crazy, he decides upon, and, for some reason, what used to make me storm out of the room and slam the door, as I did for the last few years every time he tried to see me or talk to me, now makes me stay.

I stop by your house, I have almost all my stuff in bags now, I only have to do a final cleaning and replace the things I used. I want to leave everything spotless. I feed the cats and leave. I wanted to play with the little ones but I really needed to get out of there, although everything was vibrating with an intensity conspiring to detain me and the sun was positively operatic outside.

I finished a job that was overdue. Three weeks without being able to write a single line and suddenly everything solved in an afternoon. I talked about the impact of the work in terms of the real, the real understood as body. Sometimes I have ideas. Ideas of my own that seem to be good for something.

What I don't like about high-rise buildings is that they give me vertigo. My dad lives on a twentieth floor, or it looked like a twentieth floor, I wasn't paying close attention. After a whole life spent at ground level my chest clouds up at heights. It all gets worse if I've got something in my hand, an irrational fear that things will get away from me, slip and fall.

Submarine

You tell me you see everything as if you're under water. It makes you function but at the same time it leaves you there, behind glass.

I didn't sleep at your house last night either; I felt like watching TV but the screen on yours had been shattered and I'd received no instructions about it. I wanted to just space out and channel surf but the expansion of on-demand technologies has made it almost impossible to switch off one's will and just browse. I didn't want to have to decide anything, to be responsible for deciding.

After lunch I came here. The cats decided to destroy a pillow and made a mess. I vacuumed everywhere, I want to return everything spotlessly clean.

The possibility of a job suddenly came up. I beefed up my CV with a few consistent lies, I haven't been an employee for years. It's nonspecific assistance work, like all administrative jobs. Easy hours and the money's enough to keep my head above water.

This time the cat went crazy while I was handling a knife. I kept calm. Anything that tends toward catastrophe puts me on high alert. I can hear the neighbors just beyond the door. Murmuring.

Bridges

This time I went to his place, it's a small one-bedroom in Recoleta. He has an impressive record collection, he didn't seem to have room for much else. We listened to *Frampton Comes Alive*. I didn't tell him it was the soundtrack of the childhood trips with my parents, that and *Brothers in Arms* by Dire Straits.

I don't know if it's because he saw me zoned out, with my eyes glazed over, but he treated me more gently than ever, subtly morphing the conversation into a version of truth or dare in which you get to hear the questions first, easier both to ask about and to avoid some discomfiting topics. Why are you the one who has to stay at his house? I don't know. I really didn't, I wasn't trying to be evasive. But I don't get it, doesn't he have a family? Couldn't they take care of the cats?

This morning when I was going to deposit a check at a bank near the Hilton, the sudden sensation of an island. At moments like that I'm unable to act, every possible decision is fraught, the potential consequences ramify and none seems to coincide with my objectives. I'm a machine pushed to its limits and I've crashed. Looking down at the brown water with the iridescent slick that the ships' fuel leaves behind I couldn't bring myself to cross the bridge. Is the reason we're not together that you really don't like me that much? Did you save me by leaving me? Or would I rather be her?

Sex was complicated. I can't, you said at the end, I can't have sex with you, and I asked what that meant. You said it the night you told me I love you and then you claimed that I was the one who'd said it. I can't. What are you going to do? you also said the night you stopped that spiteful cab; nothing, I'm going home.

So what actually happened? Did he hurt her? I don't know, I say, I don't know any details and I'm confused. But yes, I don't know how, I don't know with what, but there was blood in crevices between the floor tiles, on the towels that I washed with disconcerting love and devotion, thinking that cleaning them would exonerate you of something. And now it's me who's afraid, and more of myself than of you.

I decided to call her. She's OK but she doesn't want to know anything, she's OK but she doesn't want to come back here. She agreed that I bring her a few things she listed in an email. You shouldn't have to help that son of a bitch anymore. It hits me like a slow-motion punch in the gut while my brain fills in the blanks at the speed of a cheetah.

Lianas

We're playing on the bank of a nineteenth-century river. A river out of a painting. The river where Alice first heard the stories that she'd inspired. Some small and very green leaves similar to oregano are floating on the surface. My parents are there as a presiding spirit but not in the flesh, no one's waiting for us on shore as we enter the placid water, which, as soon as we get in, begins to flow and then pick up momentum. You're a tiny cat and I don't want you to get wet—I remember with terror the day my mom put Ziggy in the pool because he was dirty—but you're also waiting for me inside the old house, the quarters of an English social club that's also a faculty department and the premises of a fencing society. There's a high school band festival with names like Mantra and Bleeding Peach. Clinging to a liana or the pylon of a disintegrated dock I'm pleading for something or begging forgiveness and a dark figure out of a totally different aesthetic with a different sort of gravity, a Harry Potter film, pulls me up onto the bank and makes me promise never to enter the water so heedlessly like that again: It's just that the river changed completely once I was in it, the leaves had been still, I couldn't foresee it. But before I can finish explaining myself he disappears. I was going to change clothes before returning to the festival, at which, in the middle of a white but still rustic salon, we're going to read poetry. My neighborhood is in a coastal village, I know that my house was on the other side, it has the familiar surroundings, but in the depths of my mind I can sense that something's off. Although it's beautiful and promises a consumer paradise—New York–style cafés, bike paths that slope so there's no need to pedal, department stores with nice selections of dresses—I feel nostalgic in this Costa Esperanza, as if the sudden apparition of the promised city of childhood no longer coincides with my desires, indeed it strikes me as absolutely inappropriate. Once I get home the familiar sensation of a gray and humid Buenos Aires returns and calms me down, a message from Juan inviting me to the pool in Rio de Janeiro. I accept although deep down I know that I'll be going back to that white festival. And that's what happens; walking through the gardens a classmate from grammar school calls down to me from a window, her voice is strange, as if her mouth were numb, and she laughs, she laughs a lot, she's wearing pajamas and the clubhouse is a hospital, the white room isn't a poetry reading but a room for playing board games and you're sitting on the floor convinced that the festival that isn't going to happen will be the best one ever. The kitten is a kitten again, orange and fluffy and very tiny. I dote on him convinced that there's a conscience in there; I say things like love me again and you don't love me anymore, and for some reason I can't take him with me, and I suffer thinking that he's so little to be living all alone. Then I remember that my mom used to say cats are better than dogs because they're independent. But I was upset because the kitten despised me, despised me with his eyes and made a haughty gesture with his head, pointedly ignoring me.

Fireworks

The leg wound is almost gone, there are only a few little scabs left, I came to make everything ready for your return. The light-colored cat has just learned to climb down the stairs, now he repeats it trying to perfect his technique. I'm proud of him. The plan for Christmas is to luxuriate in the nimbus of the air conditioner watching movies and eating pizza.

The day we tickled each other I thought everything was going to be OK forever. Then you started with the yes-no, yes-no. I can't, I can't. I was fixated on the hope that you'd finally settle on yes, pretending I didn't know that you never really wanted to.

I put together the things Violeta had asked for, the mug with a rainbow on it, some Caran d'Ache markers, her collage from the living-room wall, a tin containing rings and other trinkets, a black velvet handbag embroidered with orange flowers. Don't worry about the clothing, there's not much left, I already took almost everything, same goes for the books. And I don't care about the rest, I don't want it. I followed her instructions. I'd like to be able to dispose of my own remnants so decisively. I'm not going to leave anything, but that's for my own sake, so nothing of me is left with you; if I wanted to torment you it might be different.

I'm waiting for Francisco to pick me up. I'm taking advantage of his car to move everything. What I like about having so few things, I realize now that I'm putting them back where they belong, is the feeling that there was a coherence to my choices, a guiding aesthetic. During dinner I have the nagging feeling that I left a window open at your house, imaginary tongues of flame. I wanted to go back, it's only twenty blocks, but he says no, nothing's going to happen, that it's highly unlikely that an ember is going to float in through a ground-floor window. Plus, with the inflation no one's going to be doing fireworks this year anyway. I picture the bed on fire, the cats suffocating, the floor ablaze, everything flammable surges to mind.

I never had extravagant Christmas celebrations, I don't understand the family protocol, the decorations. Ana usually visits old friends or former lovers in Europe. She always figures out a way to get back there and, to my mind, that's how she imbues herself with that elegant air she needs to sustain in order to distinguish herself from the rest of us.

After midnight, even though it seems ridiculous, he offers to drive me over to check on the window and see the cats. The feeling that I could spend my whole life with him is burning inside me because love is, perhaps, something similar to just accompanying your partner even when you think it's ridiculous. At that moment I love him, it's like a firework; or maybe it's not him per se, maybe it's just a very clear idea of how I want certain things to be from now on.

Keys Open Doors

I realize only now that I should attach your key chain to mine so I won't risk forgetting your keys in another bag the way I did the first few days. The street is empty, sun and green, lots of sun and green. The light passes through the leaves, casting natural patterns on the ground. Here and there a business is open, the produce shop on your corner, for instance.

I saw my reflection in the glass door of your living room and I was startled. I thought it was a ghost. My skirt flew up and I mistook the fluttering for an apparition.

Francisco is moving some things that were still at his parents' place, I offer to help him. He invites me to share some Christmas leftovers. Turns out I have my own technique for folding T-shirts. Nobody ever told me I was a practical person before; I like this possible me.

Stone Lions

You've entered one of those phases of not answering again, you always made it difficult to maintain continuity. I would dedicate lines from songs to you: "I don't think you're what you seem," for example, or "Every day my confusion grows." I don't feel the confusion anymore, it's more the unfairness that impresses me. A logic without logic, my psychoanalyst once called it, the unhealthy place, the shackles of habit. I'm skeptical of diseases, I think they're more like a lack of drive.

You'll be back soon. But you're only coming back to a house, there's no more normal. The knives are going to be there, the cats, and the remains of a relationship. You're going to keep chain-smoking. I was here taking care of your cats, your frayed cables, making sure the doors didn't fall off their hinges, and now you won't answer. At a certain point the body becomes what you hold onto in order to survive, last night I started by folding T-shirts.

After the movies we went to play pool. I told him I hardly know how to play but that I was willing to make a fool of myself. My dad taught me one summer, he said I was a natural. It was at the weekend house of some friends he had in San Diego. I was never nuts about gated communities, they seem fictional to me. Stone lions, unlocked doors, very blond children on bicycles.

I can't sleep in your bed anymore so this morning we came back here. Fran fell asleep on my chest telling me his thoughts about *Star Wars*, it addresses basic human concerns, he says.

It's like Greek theater. It's politics. It moves us because it touches on the truth: The darkness is within us.

In the middle of the night I wake up with the recurring nightmare. I find my mother sprawled out again on the floor, a frothy drool oozing from her mouth. This time, instead of becoming a little girl, I run away from home and run, run and nothing makes sense, disparate images streaming by, all the people I've met in my life, my mother is my mother, but it's you and she doesn't seem kind, a suddenly repugnant creature. I wake up with the feeling that she's died, a feeling much more real than all the times she died in my dreams after she died in real life.

My room was always the hottest in the house. The sun bakes the tin roof and the breeze can't negotiate the acute angle between the window and the dividing wall. My mom was convinced that children shouldn't have air-conditioning, that it was bad for their lungs, and I, as a girl, as a baby, had a disease that I don't remember, a pneumonia that resolved itself without any long-term consequences but which had been very hard on her. The ceiling fan broke, I don't know when; without any warning it just stopped working at some point, maybe it happened when I wasn't here. Actually, anything I say at this point would be a lie. It's been there forever, motionless. It's white and pink.

I wake him up, we're both drenched. I suggest that we sleep in the office, which has a twin bed, but I reconsider and we go to her room, which has air-conditioning and is almost completely emptied out by now. It's the first time I've slept there since she killed herself.

We leave in a hurry, he continues moving stuff while I go out to replace a few things of yours that I used. At the supermarket I ask for a bottle of Havana Club from the glass cabinet, I buy two mineral waters, the pink liquid you use to clean the floors, and a loaf of sliced white bread. The cashier remarks that the rum is a bit expensive, that it's Cuban, I tell him I have no choice. I have no choice because I won't tolerate failure, although I could just walk away from the whole thing and, what's more, make off with the dark chocolate, the perfumes and paintings, and some of the guitars as well, all the guitars.

I gather up the last things, my toothbrush, my hairbrush, my shower brush, makeup remover pads, contact lens case. I stick them all in a resealable plastic pouch that I put inside my shoulder bag, the canvas one from the Parisian bookstore where I bought the copy of *Pour en finir avec le jugement de dieu* for you, Juan's suggestion.

Then I found out you didn't know French and I felt bad, but it was Juan's idea, he said you were going to love it. And somehow you did, because you put it in a visible place on your bookshelf; now suddenly it's not there, I couldn't find it. Violeta put it somewhere or threw it away, or maybe you did yourself during one of your attacks. The book had been damaged anyway. The day I returned from Paris, when I was on my way to see you, the bag in which I was carrying it slipped through the grid of the bicycle basket and got caught in the spokes of the front wheel. I managed to brake in time to avoid flying headfirst over the handlebars onto the pavement but the book was mangled, practically split down the middle.

I go back to my house to take a shower and put on a dress and some makeup. When it's this muggy you have to shower at least twice a day.

Fran invited me to the birthday party of a friend of his, a rooftop with an incredible view on the twenty-fifth floor. He says I don't have to be afraid of his friends, that I shouldn't have any preconceptions, he doesn't believe that what I actually fear is heights. Just come, nobody's going to force you to look down.

We dance and kiss each other and the sunrise is pink and orange. The drinks are pink and orange, too, and brown. I don't understand Coca-Cola: How can we knowingly drink something that's used for cleaning screws? Someone invites us to share a line, we decide not to and then take a cab home. First we stop at a newsstand and buy all sorts of frivolous nonsense, the lollipops that come with a powder that explodes in your mouth, gummy alphabet letters, and a bottle of sparkling water that I grabbed by mistake. But it doesn't matter, we laugh at the bubbles, how they tingle on the palate. All so effervescent and none of it will last.

Last Things

Your message wakes me up. How's it going there? I'm coming back to myself, you say. You want to leave. In any case, it's done. It's today.

I go out to the yard to water the plants, take the clothes off the clothesline. An orange butterfly with black spots is resting flat on the ground next to the potted azalea. Can it be true that they live for only a day? How can collectors bear the dead beauty? Restoring an insect. Shiny wings and bent like a fiction. The simulation of plenitude behind glass.

I go through the shelves one by one, retrieving a few odd things, a handkerchief, a book, tampons, a vest, some palo santo. I'm suffocating in the heat so I lie down for a few minutes on the cool cement floor, flattening my whole back against it. I'm exhausted. The cats stop playing among themselves and come closer, they climb up my legs. I pick up the lighter-colored one by the scruff of his neck, put him on my chest and tell him the truth: I'm going to miss you.

A scratching noise on the wood up above interrupts my confession, an enormous bug is trying to squeeze through a crevice between the ceiling and the paneled wall. From the intensity of it I was expecting to see a rat, or maybe a bat. I'm not going to kill it, I decide, still frightened and scuttling toward the other side of the room; I won't be battling any insect prodigies today. And I block out the sounds of its scratching.

I fill up their bowls in case you're late—I can't wait around for you—leave the keys in the glass ashtray, bathroom light switched on so you won't step on the kittens when you arrive. Using both arms, I carry out the last of my things. The hallway is dark, as usual.

A highly regarded poet, MALÉN DENIS is an Argentine multidisciplinary artist and nonacademic philosopher who lives in New York and Barcelona. She has contributed essays to *Nylon, The Washington Post,* and *Architectural Digest,* and her art has been commissioned by the National Autonomous University in Mexico and the Museum of Modern Art of Buenos Aires.

LAURA HATRY received a PhD in Hispanic studies from the Autónoma de Madrid; she is an independent researcher and translator.

JOHN WRONOSKI is a scholar, rare-book consultant, and specialist in the appraisal and sale of literary archives.

New Directions Paperbooks—a partial listing

Adonis, Songs of Mihyar the Damascene
César Aira, Ghosts
An Episode in the Life of a Landscape Painter
Ryunosuke Akutagawa, Kappa
Will Alexander, Refractive Africa
Osama Alomar, The Teeth of the Comb
Guillaume Apollinaire, Selected Writings
Jessica Au, Cold Enough for Snow
Paul Auster, The Red Notebook
Ingeborg Bachmann, Malina
Honoré de Balzac, Colonel Chabert
Djuna Barnes, Nightwood
Charles Baudelaire, The Flowers of Evil*
Bei Dao, City Gate, Open Up
Yevgenia Belorusets, Lucky Breaks
Rafael Bernal, His Name Was Death
Mei-Mei Berssenbrugge, Empathy
Max Blecher, Adventures in Immediate Irreality
Jorge Luis Borges, Labyrinths
Seven Nights
Coral Bracho, Firefly Under the Tongue*
Kamau Brathwaite, Ancestors
Anne Carson, Glass, Irony & God
Wrong Norma
Horacio Castellanos Moya, Senselessness
Camilo José Cela, Mazurka for Two Dead Men
Louis-Ferdinand Céline
Death on the Installment Plan
Journey to the End of the Night
Inger Christensen, alphabet
Julio Cortázar, Cronopios and Famas
Jonathan Creasy (ed.), Black Mountain Poems
Robert Creeley, If I Were Writing This
H.D., Selected Poems
Guy Davenport, 7 Greeks
Amparo Dávila, The Houseguest
Osamu Dazai, The Flowers of Buffoonery
No Longer Human
The Setting Sun
Anne de Marcken
It Lasts Forever and Then It's Over
Helen DeWitt, The Last Samurai
Some Trick
José Donoso, The Obscene Bird of Night
Robert Duncan, Selected Poems
Eça de Queirós, The Maias
Juan Emar, Yesterday
William Empson, 7 Types of Ambiguity
Mathias Énard, Compass
Shusaku Endo, Deep River
Jenny Erpenbeck, Go, Went, Gone
Kairos
Lawrence Ferlinghetti
A Coney Island of the Mind
Thalia Field, Personhood
F. Scott Fitzgerald, The Crack-Up
Rivka Galchen, Little Labors
Forrest Gander, Be With
Romain Gary, The Kites
Natalia Ginzburg, The Dry Heart
Henry Green, Concluding
Marlen Haushofer, The Wall
Victor Heringer, The Love of Singular Men
Felisberto Hernández, Piano Stories
Hermann Hesse, Siddhartha
Takashi Hiraide, The Guest Cat
Yoel Hoffmann, Moods
Susan Howe, My Emily Dickinson
Concordance
Bohumil Hrabal, I Served the King of England
Qurratulain Hyder, River of Fire
Sonallah Ibrahim, That Smell
Rachel Ingalls, Mrs. Caliban
Christopher Isherwood, The Berlin Stories
Fleur Jaeggy, Sweet Days of Discipline
Alfred Jarry, Ubu Roi
B.S. Johnson, House Mother Normal
James Joyce, Stephen Hero
Franz Kafka, Amerika: The Man Who Disappeared
Yasunari Kawabata, Dandelions
Mieko Kanai, Mild Vertigo
John Keene, Counternarratives
Kim Hyesoon, Autobiography of Death
Heinrich von Kleist, Michael Kohlhaas
Taeko Kono, Toddler-Hunting
László Krasznahorkai, Satantango
Seiobo There Below
Ágota Kristóf, The Illiterate
Eka Kurniawan, Beauty Is a Wound
Mme. de Lafayette, The Princess of Clèves
Lautréamont, Maldoror
Siegfried Lenz, The German Lesson
Alexander Lernet-Holenia, Count Luna

Denise Levertov, Selected Poems
Li Po, Selected Poems
Clarice Lispector, An Apprenticeship
The Hour of the Star
The Passion According to G. H.
Federico García Lorca, Selected Poems*
Nathaniel Mackey, Splay Anthem
Xavier de Maistre, Voyage Around My Room
Stéphane Mallarmé, Selected Poetry and Prose*
Javier Marías, Your Face Tomorrow (3 volumes)
Bernadette Mayer, Midwinter Day
Carson McCullers, The Member of the Wedding
Fernando Melchor, Hurricane Season
Paradais
Thomas Merton, New Seeds of Contemplation
The Way of Chuang Tzu
Henri Michaux, A Barbarian in Asia
Henry Miller, The Colossus of Maroussi
Big Sur & the Oranges of Hieronymus Bosch
Yukio Mishima, Confessions of a Mask
Death in Midsummer
Eugenio Montale, Selected Poems*
Vladimir Nabokov, Laughter in the Dark
Pablo Neruda, The Captain's Verses*
Love Poems*
Charles Olson, Selected Writings
George Oppen, New Collected Poems
Wilfred Owen, Collected Poems
Hiroko Oyamada, The Hole
José Emilio Pacheco, Battles in the Desert
Michael Palmer, Little Elegies for Sister Satan
Nicanor Parra, Antipoems*
Boris Pasternak, Safe Conduct
Octavio Paz, Poems of Octavio Paz
Victor Pelevin, Omon Ra
Fernando Pessoa
The Complete Works of Alberto Caeiro
Alejandra Pizarnik
Extracting the Stone of Madness
Robert Plunket, My Search for Warren Harding
Ezra Pound, The Cantos
New Selected Poems and Translations
Qian Zhongshu, Fortress Besieged
Raymond Queneau, Exercises in Style
Olga Ravn, The Employees
Herbert Read, The Green Child
Kenneth Rexroth, Selected Poems
Keith Ridgway, A Shock
Rainer Maria Rilke
Poems from the Book of Hours
Arthur Rimbaud, Illuminations*
A Season in Hell and The Drunken Boat*
Evelio Rosero, The Armies
Fran Ross, Oreo
Joseph Roth, The Emperor's Tomb
Raymond Roussel, Locus Solus
Ihara Saikaku, The Life of an Amorous Woman
Nathalie Sarraute, Tropisms
Jean-Paul Sartre, Nausea
Kathryn Scanlan, Kick the Latch
Delmore Schwartz
In Dreams Begin Responsibilities
W. G. Sebald, The Emigrants
The Rings of Saturn
Anne Serre, The Governesses
Patti Smith, Woolgathering
Stevie Smith, Best Poems
Novel on Yellow Paper
Gary Snyder, Turtle Island
Muriel Spark, The Driver's Seat
The Public Image
Maria Stepanova, In Memory of Memory
Wislawa Szymborska, How to Start Writing
Antonio Tabucchi, Pereira Maintains
Junichiro Tanizaki, The Maids
Yoko Tawada, The Emissary
Scattered All over the Earth
Dylan Thomas, A Child's Christmas in Wales
Collected Poems
Thuan, Chinatown
Rosemary Tonks, The Bloater
Tomas Tranströmer, The Great Enigma
Leonid Tsypkin, Summer in Baden-Baden
Tu Fu, Selected Poems
Elio Vittorini, Conversations in Sicily
Rosmarie Waldrop, The Nick of Time
Robert Walser, The Tanners
Eliot Weinberger, An Elemental Thing
Nineteen Ways of Looking at Wang Wei
Nathanael West, The Day of the Locust
Miss Lonelyhearts
Tennessee Williams, The Glass Menagerie
A Streetcar Named Desire
William Carlos Williams, Selected Poems
Alexis Wright, Praiseworthy
Louis Zukofsky, "A"

*BILINGUAL EDITION

For a complete listing, request a free catalog from New Directions, 80 8th Avenue, New York, NY 10011 or visit us online at **ndbooks.com**